03.97

'Sister Sunshine,' Adam murmured sleepily.

And then, very softly, for the first time he said her name. 'Julie.'

Her heart beat unevenly, especially knowing that he was so close to her that one movement—one small movement—and she would be in his arms. And there was nothing she could do, nothing she wanted to do, in that endless moment to stop that.

It was Adam who moved away. 'I'm sorry, Sister Maynard,' he said, his voice stiff, formal. 'I was half-asleep—I must be more tired than I thought.'

Or I wouldn't have come close to kissing you. The words were unspoken but she knew very well that that was what he was thinking. . .

Kids. . .one of life's joys, one of life's treasures.

Kisses. . .of warmth, kisses of passion, kisses from mothers and kisses from lovers.

In *Kids & Kisses*. . .every story has it all.

Elisabeth Scott was born in Scotland, but has lived in South Africa for many years. Happily married, with four children and grandchildren, she has always been interested in reading and writing about medical instances. Her middle daughter is a midwifery sister, and is Elisabeth's consultant on both medical authenticity and on how nurses feel and react. Her daughter wishes she met more doctors like the ones her mother writes about!

Recent titles by the same author:

THE DISTURBING DR SHELDON

SISTER SUNSHINE

BY
ELISABETH SCOTT

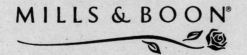

MILLS & BOON®

For my own Sister Sunshine, my daughter Heather.

*First published in Great Britain 1997
Harlequin Mills & Boon Limited,
Eton House, 18-24 Paradise Road, Richmond, Surrey TW9 1SR*

© Elisabeth Scott 1997

ISBN 0 263 80124 1

*Set in Times 10 on 11 pt. by
Rowland Phototypesetting Limited
Bury St Edmunds, Suffolk*

03-9705-52930-D

*Printed and bound in Great Britain
by Mackays of Chatham PLC, Chatham*

CHAPTER ONE

'IT's a cop-out, going to work in an old-age home!'
Julie's friend Meg said when Julie told her. 'Who on
earth will you meet there? And I'm talking about men!'

'No one,' Julie told her thankfully. 'No two-timing
doctors, no good-looking patients who think they're the
answer to a nurse's prayer. And it isn't just an old-age
home—it's more a small private geriatric hospital.'

Meg brushed that aside.

'And it's in Cape Town—you could surely have
found something here in Durban.'

'I wanted a change, in every way,' Julie said.

'You sure have got yourself one,' Meg returned. And
then, her voice softening, she said, 'Julie, I know you've
had a couple of bad experiences, but that's life. You
shouldn't run away from it.'

Julie could feel her cheeks growing warm, for Meg
had come uncomfortably close to the way she had been
thinking.

'I'm not running away,' she said quickly, defensively.
'I'm looking forward to—to a different kind of nursing.'

That, certainly, was true. She'd spent the last six
months since she'd reached the coveted Sister's badge
in charge of Men's Surgical, and before that she'd been
in Theatre. So—yes, she did feel ready for a change.

Which was what she had told the board of directors
of Halvey House at her interview.

Meg shrugged and gave in.

'Well, since I can't make you change your mind, I'll
have to wish you luck,' she said. 'I just think you don't
know what you're letting yourself in for, Julie.'

A quiet, peaceful life, that's what, Julie thought on
the long drive from Durban to Cape Town. Her little
blue Citi-Golf took the long journey in its stride, coping
with the mountain passes and the long lonely stretches
of freeway, until finally she stopped at the top of the
pass above Gordon's Bay—with Table Mountain shimmering in the heat ahead of her and the blue sea
stretching out across False Bay.

And the apprehension she had been feeling about the
wisdom of her choice faded away. She drove down the
pass, singing, 'I love to go a-wandering. . .' at the top
of her voice.

Oh, yes, she thought thankfully a little more than an
hour later as she turned into the drive of Halvey House,
this is what I want. A quiet, peaceful life—away from
places and people I know.

She was pleased that she had managed to find her
way here for she had come for the first time on the day
of her interview, and this old part of Cape Town, right
on the slopes of Table Mountain, was confusing.

The gracious, sprawling old Victorian house, set in
its large grounds, was as charming as she remembered
it. She stood on the wide, shady stoep when she had
rung the bell and looked down at Cape Town, spread
out below her between the mountain and the sea.

Rather to her surprise, it was Matron herself who
opened the door.

'I saw you drive up, Sister Maynard,' she said, shaking Julie's hand. 'Welcome to Halvey House. I was so
much hoping you wouldn't change your mind about
coming to us.'

She led Julie into her office, and lifted the phone to
ask for tea.

'I'm sure you can do with it,' she said comfortably.
'Then you can get settled in.'

The letter of appointment had said that there would

be a small flat for her on the premises, and that was one
of the aspects which had appealed to Julie, having lived
some distance from the big hospital in Durban.

A little later, delighted, she looked out of the window
under the eaves down into the garden.

'It's not much more than a bedsitter, really,' Matron
apologised. 'You do have an electric kettle and there's
a toaster inside the cupboard, but you'll have your meals
in the staff dining-room.'

She looked at her watch.

'I'll have to leave you, my dear—it's time for Dr
Brent's round. You know where to find the dining-room,
and the floor you're in charge of is right below this. I'll
see you tomorrow.'

Dr Brent's round. Julie hadn't met him as he'd been
away on a course when she'd had her interview, but
Matron had mentioned that he was a widower. Julie
pictured him as a little like her father, probably. Kindly
and grey-haired—opting for a quiet life with his elderly
patients.

She unpacked and set out her uniform, ready for
morning. She arranged her photographs on the dressing
table—her mother and father, her brothers with their
surfboards, the old dog, Glen and her graduation picture.
And that was all.

She had thrown out her other photos before she left
Durban. Tim Curran with his arm around her—casually,
possessively—at the Hospital Ball. Mark Elliott turning
from the wheel of his yacht and smiling as she took the
picture.

'They're not worth wasting a moment's thought on,
neither of them,' Meg had said firmly. 'There are plenty
more pebbles on the beach.'

No, thank you, Julie thought now, remembering. I
don't want any more pebbles, not for a long, long time—
they just make the beach too stony!

For a moment, with a pang, she wished that Meg or Hilary or Jane was around to share that with and smile. It was all very well leaving the hospital, leaving Durban, but suddenly it dawned on her just what leaving her friends and her family meant.

Come on, cheer up, she told herself severely as she caught sight of herself in the mirror. Determinedly she smiled, and the girl in the mirror smiled back—a smile that took a little while to reach the wide brown eyes.

She pinned that smile on again next morning when she was ready to take charge of her ward. Dressed in her blue uniform—short-sleeved for summer—with her epaulettes, her badge and her fob watch, she looked responsible and professional, she told herself reassuringly. It did still sometimes surprise her that she was actually a sister now, and she pinned up an unruly blonde curl which was threatening to ruin this picture.

The night sister, Sister Anderson, was pleasant and welcoming.

'I always have a cup of coffee just before I leave— thought you'd like one too,' she said.

She smiled.

'You'll find things rather different from working in a big city hospital, Sister Maynard,' she said. 'We do have some patients who are here for just a few weeks, but most of our folks are here permanently. They need more actual medical care than they could get in an old-age home but they also need a place with more warmth and comfort than a hospital, and that's what we give them. And that means the whole atmosphere is just a bit more casual and relaxed.'

She told Julie a little about the patients on the second floor, handed over the keys to the drug cupboard and explained where the patients' files were kept.

When she left Julie took a deep breath, straightened

her shoulders and got into this first day at Halvey House.

The morning routine, she found, was reassuringly familiar. The breakfast trolley arrived and Julie and her young assistant, Prudence Solomon, gave out the breakfasts. Then there were dressings to be changed, medication to be sorted out for the day, charts to fill in, a hip replacement patient to be helped to walk in a frame and a rheumatoid arthritis patient to be supervised while she did her exercises.

'Because she won't, unless we stand over her,' Prudence explained. 'The physiotherapist comes once a week, but Miss Clifford is suppposed to do her exercises every day.'

Miss Clifford was small and bird-like, with snowy-white hair beautifully pinned up at the back of her head. Captain O'Connor's Irish accent was still strong, although he told Julie that he had left Dublin fifty years ago. Mrs Smit—Ted Ramsay—Mrs Ngalo—

'I'll get them all sorted out,' Julie said to Prudence as they were having coffee in the middle of the morning in the tiny duty room which served as Julie's office, linen cupboard and drug cupboard. 'When does Dr Brent have his round?'

'Oh, there's no set time,' Prudence told her. 'I think he's at the City Clinic today—he does anaesthetics there once or twice a week. It all depends how long that takes; he'll probably look in in the afternoon.'

She stood up.

'All right if I help Miss Clifford to bath now?' she asked. 'She's a little less stiff by late morning, and the warm bath does help.'

Julie said that she would take the chance to go over the files and become familiar with them, then she wanted to spend some time with each of her patients.

She had reached Ted Ramsay's file, and was reading about the onset of his illness—multiple sclerosis—when she slowly became aware that she wasn't alone. She looked up.

Afterwards, when she thought about that first meeting with Dr Adam Brent she could never get away from the immediate and dismaying feeling of disapproval she'd sensed, and that before she'd even known who he was.

'You are Sister Maynard?' he said, and there was surprise in his voice. And then, as she looked at him, he went on impatiently, 'I'm Dr Brent, Sister.'

He was younger than she had expected—probably mid-thirties, Julie thought, and certainly not the kindly, grey-haired man she had been expecting. Just as it was all too clear that she wasn't what he had been expecting.

'Dr Brent,' she said, standing up, annoyed at herself for feeling—and, she was certain, looking—more than a little thrown. 'We weren't expecting you until this afternoon.'

'Dr Hutton was ill; he cancelled some of his theatre list.'

His grey eyes were cool.

'You're—younger than I expected,' he said abruptly.

Julie felt her cheeks grow warm.

'I'm twenty-six,' she replied, knowing that she sounded defensive. And I've had my sister's badge for six months, she wanted to add. He shrugged, dismissing that.

'I gather you have no geriatric experience?' he said.

'No, I haven't,' Julie agreed. She took a deep, steadying breath. 'But I do have experience in every branch of nursing that is relevant and, as I told the board of directors, I look on my patients as people first. Age is irrelevant.'

'Nice sentiment, but rather naïve and ill-informed,' the doctor returned. 'With many of our patients, the course and prognosis of their illnesses are directly affected by the fact that they are no longer young. Which I would have pointed out if I had been at your interview. Unfortunately I had to be away.'

Unfortunately? His meaning was all too clear. If he had been there he wouldn't have supported her appointment.

Julie lifted her chin but just in time she held back the hot words of defence, the statement that neither Matron nor the board had found either her youth or her lack of geriatric experience a bar.

'I'll come round the patients with you right now, Dr Brent,' she said, her voice as cool as his.

'No need,' he told her. 'I just want to check Ted Ramsay's new medication and have a word with Mrs Ngalo. I'll be back in to see the others this afternoon.'

Julie went back to her files, but she was so angry that it was a little while before she could calm down enough to concentrate.

A little later, to her surprise, she heard laughter from Ted Ramsay's room, and when she glanced up the doctor was still smiling as he walked past. But the smile disappeared—as if it had been switched off, Julie thought—as he passed her. He nodded brusquely, and strode on past the lift to the wide staircase.

'What's with the doctor?' Julie asked Prudence when there was a quiet time after lunch, with some of the patients having visitors and others having a sleep. 'He made it very clear that he thinks I'm too young and too inexperienced for the job. He could at least give me a chance; wait to see how I do first.'

The younger girl looked surprised. 'He's very nice— Dr Brent,' she said. 'The patients are fond of him, and— and he's always been easy to work with. Not that I have much to do with him—I'm only a nurse-aide— but Sister Carter got on well with him.'

'And how old was Sister Carter?' Julie asked, pretty certain what the answer would be.

Prudence smiled, her dark eyes lighting up the smooth brown skin.

'She was sixty when she retired,' she said demurely. She held out both hands wide. 'And she was this size.' Then, her smile fading, she said, 'Maybe he just had a bad day, and took it out on you, Sister Maynard. It can't be easy for him, bringing up two kids on his own.'

Dr Brent's wife had been killed in a car accident almost two years ago, she told Julie, and his children were still small.

'Catherine is seven, I think, and the little boy, David, is only five. They're not here at the moment; they're with Dr Brent's parents. But maybe it does just get a bit much for him sometimes, and you were unfortunate enough to get the rough edge of that. Give him a chance—he's really a nice man.'

He may be, Julie thought, but I didn't see much sign of that, and he certainly didn't give me much of a chance. On the other hand, I have to work with him, so I suppose I shouldn't let myself dwell on how he was today. Maybe he did have a bad day—maybe he'll be different next time I see him.

But there was no sign of any thaw in Dr Brent's manner in the next few days. He was polite and professional—but cool and distant.

Everyone else at Halvey House was so pleasant and so welcoming that it didn't really matter, Julie told herself. She didn't have to see much of him for although he lived in a cottage in the grounds of the big house there was a separate gate. But it rankled that he wasn't even prepared to give her a chance—to see how competent she was at her job—before deciding that she was too young to do it properly.

The first floor sister, Brenda Morkel, told her at lunch one day that Adam Brent was thirty-six. 'I knew him when we were both training at Groote Schuur,' she said.

'Not well—Adam wasn't in the same crowd—but it was nice to find him here when I came four years ago. His little boy, David, is the same age as my Helen and they go to the same nursery school.'

She hesitated. 'I think,' she said slowly, 'that Adam has changed since his wife died. Not to folks he knows; folks he feels comfortable with. But he probably does tend to keep himself to himself now. I wouldn't take it personally, Julie, the way you say he is with you.'

And that is good advice, Julie told herself. She didn't, in fact, believe that it was true, for she was quite certain that Adam Brent's dislike of her was all too personal. But it was no good dwelling on it, she would do her job and do it well, and she certainly wouldn't waste any time worrying about what Dr Adam Brent thought of her.

She was getting to know her patients slowly. There were a dozen of them on her floor, and by the end of the first week she had been able to spend some time each day with each one of them.

Captain O'Connor was an entertaining, cheerful man and she loved his Irish accent, even though she suspected that he put it on a bit for her benefit.

'Sure and it's lucky I am that I can see the sea from my window,' he said to her one morning when she was changing the dressing on a small ulcer on his leg. 'Many a time have I not sailed into Table Bay in the years gone by, and me never thinking it would be here that I would end my days.'

'Did you not want to go back to Ireland, Captain?' Julie asked, deftly putting gauze over the small ulcer. The old man shook his head.

'I was in Cape Town when the stroke hit me,' he told her, 'and me within a year of retiring. There's few of my own folks left in Dublin now, and I can get my pension just as well here. It's enough to let me stay on.

Sure and Halvey House has become as much home to me as any place has, other than the cabin of my ship.'

He had never married, he told her. And with a glint in his blue eyes—faded a little now, Julie thought, but surely once the colour of the sea he loved so much—he said, 'I wouldn't exactly be saying I had a girl in every port but, well, now, there were plenty ports and enough girls, and it was a grand life. So grand that the years just crept by, and me with never a thought of settling down. By the time I did think of it, all these lovely girls had found someone else to settle down with.'

He looked beyond her. 'It's yourself, Doctor,' he said. 'We're just after having a nice little chat here, me and Sister.'

Adam Brent smiled and Julie thought, a little unwillingly, how much nicer he looked when he smiled. Not nearly so reserved and forbidding.

'I think you would be doing most of the talking, Captain.'

'Aye, that would be the way of it,' the old man agreed.

The doctor's smile disappeared. 'I'd like a word with you, Sister,' he said.

Julie followed him to the small duty room and stood at the door, her hands clasped correctly as she waited for him to speak.

'That ulcer isn't healing,' he said, and he frowned. 'I think we're going to have to consider a skin graft.'

'His circulation is so poor,' Julie said. 'And on his shin—would a skin graft take, Dr Brent?'

'I'm not too hopeful,' the doctor admitted. 'Keep on with the dressings and that new cream for a week, Sister, and we'll see how it looks then.'

When he had gone Julie made a note in the captain's file. There was no doubt, she thought with some reluctance, that she couldn't fault Dr Adam Brent professionally. And he wasn't in any way distant with the patients, and that was what really mattered.

That night she finished the letter she was writing to Meg.

You asked in your letter—and you're a dear, to write so quickly—about the doctor here. Well, I can promise you I'm in no danger from him. You know the kind of man I keep falling for—tall, dark and handsome, and full of charm. Dr Adam Brent isn't very tall, he's got brown hair and he's very ordinary. And he has NO CHARM. Added to that, he thinks I'm too young for my job, and he's made it very clear that if he'd been around he would have seen to it that I didn't get it!

With some satisfaction she licked the stamp, and wrote Meg's address on the envelope.

Little Miss Clifford had already become another of her favourite patients. She was small and bird-like, and although her hands were swollen and knotted she managed to pin up her silvery hair perfectly.

'Your hair always looks so nice,' Julie said to her one day.

'I've always worn it like this,' Miss Clifford said. 'We had to, you see, for the stage. I was a ballerina, Sister.' Her voice was full of pride.

Julie looked at the pictures on the wall. 'I could see you were interested in ballet,' she said. 'Margot Fonteyn—Markova—Spira—Nureyev. Are there any pictures of you dancing?'

'I don't need pictures when I have my memories,' the old lady said. 'I could have danced at Covent Garden, you know, but I chose to stay here and dance in Cape Town. Oh, my dear, if you could only have seen me dance Odette/Odile! Do you like ballet?'

'Yes, I love it,' Julie replied. 'Like many little girls,

I did go to ballet but I suppose I wasn't much good—
we're more into sports in my family.'

'What a pity,' Miss Clifford murmured. 'Let me see
you do a pirouette.'

I must have been out of my mind, Julie thought afterwards. Whatever possessed me to do what she said, right
there, and me in uniform and on duty? She had been
halfway through the requested pirouette when the door
opened and Adam Brent came in. And the look on his
face said all too clearly that this confirmed all his doubts
about the suitability of Sister Maynard.

'Am I interrupting something, Sister Maynard?' Dr
Brent asked politely and coolly. Julie managed, somehow, to regain her balance. But not her dignity, nor her
composure.

'Dr Brent,' she began, not sure what she was going
to say—not sure what she wanted to say.

'Don't be angry with Sister Maynard, Dr Brent,' Miss
Clifford said anxiously. 'I asked her to do a pirouette
for me, you see.'

The doctor's grey eyes—grey, and cold as the sea on
a winter's day, Julie thought, her heart sinking even
further—studied Julie thoughtfully.

'I'm not angry,' he said after a moment. 'I'm not
even surprised. Sister Maynard, I'd like to have another
look at Captain O'Connor's leg, if you can spare
the time.'

His voice changed, and he smiled as he looked down
at the silver-haired old lady. 'And don't you go leading
Sister Maynard astray, Miss Clifford. This is not the
time or the place for ballet performances.'

Julie followed him along the corridor to the captain's
room, wishing desperately that she had had the sense
not to give in to that impulse. But she said nothing.
Silence, she thought, might not have been golden, but
it was probably the safest policy right now.

'Ahoy there, Dr Brent,' the captain said cheerfully. 'Parade time, I'll be bound.'

'Yes, parade time, Captain,' Adam Brent agreed. 'Let's have a look at your leg, then. Sister?'

Deftly and gently Julie took the bandage off the old man's leg, knowing all too well that there was no improvement in the small ulcerated wound on his shin. The doctor's big brown hands touched the old man's leg sensitively, watching—Julie knew—for signs of swelling around the ulcerated area.

'I had hopes for that new enzyme treatment,' he said at last, and Julie was relieved to see that the cool appraisal in his eyes had gone.

'Every time I changed the dressing I was hoping I'd see pink healthy tissue,' she said.

'Sorry, Captain,' the doctor said then, 'but we're going to have to do something more with this. I'll fix things with Dr Hutton at the Clinic and we'll have a skin graft done.'

The old man's white bushy eyebrows drew together. 'You'll not get me staying there,' he said fiercely. 'I don't mind if they do the job but I'll be coming back to my own bed here, Dr Brent.' Looking at the doctor, Julie could see that this wasn't entirely unexpected.

'I know you didn't like it last time, Captain,' Adam Brent said carefully, 'but it would only be for a day or two so that Dr Hutton could see how you were doing.'

'Sure and he can come here and see how I'm doing, and him with that fine big German car,' the old man said. He folded his arms, and looked steadily at Adam Brent. 'You tell him, Doctor, that between you and Sister Sunshine I'll do just fine here.'

'Sister Sunshine?' Adam Brent said, quite clearly taken aback.

Julie could feel her cheeks growing warm.

'And doesn't she bring sunshine into all our lives, and

her with her golden hair and always a smile?' Captain
O'Connor demanded. 'That's what we call her, me and
Miss Clifford and Mrs Smit.'

'Ah, your two lady friends,' the doctor said,
recovering a little. 'Well, we'll have to see what Dr
Hutton says—I'm not making any promises.'

'And neither am I, Dr Brent,' the old captain returned
blandly. 'No promises at all, unless he does it the way
I want.'

Adam Brent and Julie walked back along the corridor
and the doctor, she was relieved to see, was still smiling.

'He's a dreadful old man,' he said, affection in his
voice, 'but I half expected this so I've already talked to
Ken Hutton. They'll do the skin graft, and he can be
back here the same day.'

In the duty room he picked up Captain O'Connor's
folder. 'We've been lucky with the old boy,' he said.
'Since the cerebral embolism he's been on anti-
coagulant drugs, and there's been no further embolism.
All right, his left side is still badly impaired, but he says
himself he'd rather need his wheelchair to get around
than have problems with his speech.'

'So he didn't lose his speech at all?' Julie asked.

'A temporary loss of function in the first couple of
days,' the doctor told her. 'We had a speech therapist
in right away—his company arranged for him to come
here as soon as he was out of Intensive Care. There was
no serious damage to the speech centre of the brain,
fortunately. But the circulation in that leg is pretty poor,
in spite of physiotherapy, and that's why we haven't
had any success with this ulcerated wound.' He
straightened up.

'Thank you, Sister,' he said, his voice formal again.
'I'll let you know what we arrange for him.'

He hadn't made any comment about the Sister
Sunshine business, Julie thought when he had gone, but

she was pretty sure he would disapprove of that as much as he had obviously disapproved of her little ballet performance.

And all at once the funny side of that struck her— Adam Brent coming into the room to find the sister-in-charge twirling round, her skirt lifted high in a most unseemly manner. She wished now that she had seen the astonishment on his face in that first moment before it became cold and disapproving and she couldn't help smiling, thinking of that. He had looked surprised enough hearing her called Sister Sunshine. Nice, that, she thought appreciatively. No matter what Dr Brent thought of it!

The bell rang from Mrs Ngalo's room, and she hurried to answer it as Prudence was at lunch, and already she knew that the quiet lady in Room Six never rang unless she had to.

Mrs Ngalo was one of the short-term patients, here to recuperate after a hip replacement. Julie and Prudence had got her out of bed to sit in a high-backed chair at the window, which she was supposed to do for half an hour at a time, but Julie could see that the twenty minutes or so had been long enough.

'I am sorry, Sister,' Mrs Ngalo murmured apologetically, 'but I would like to be back in bed now.'

'Of course, Mrs Ngalo,' Julie said, and she helped her patient back to bed, placing a pillow between her knees when she was lying on her side to prevent possible dislocation of the hip before the soft tissue had had a chance to heal.

'More comfortable now?' she asked, and the older woman nodded.

'Your family will be here soon,' Julie said. 'They never miss visiting time.'

'They feel it is wrong for me to be here at all,' Mrs Ngalo said. 'In our culture old people are looked after

by the family. My daughters and my daughters-in-law
would rather have me at home, but the doctor who did
the operation said I must come here for a few weeks.'

'Your doctor was right. You need nursing care, and
you need therapy,' Julie replied, moving a glass of water
within her patient's reach. She smiled. 'You're not
exactly old, you know—you're one of our youngest
patients.' Shyly, the woman returned her smile.

'I am sixty-one,' she said, 'and I have nine grandchildren. Perhaps when I can walk again I will bring
some of them here to visit you. The older ones come,
but not the babies.'

'I would like that,' Julie said, 'but I don't see why
the little ones shouldn't come to visit you—I'll have a
word with Matron.' She was relieved to see that her
patient looked better now, and she made a mental note
to tell the phsyiotherapist that half an hour was, perhaps,
too long out of bed at this stage.

And as she thought that she remembered what Adam
Brent had said at their first meeting. Age, he had said,
wasn't irrelevant. The fact that a patient was no longer
young, would undoubtedly have an effect on their
recovery.

She could see that that was true for Mrs Ngalo. If she
had had a hip replacement done ten or fifteen years ago
she would have recovered more quickly. And if she'd
been ten years older it might have taken her longer.

So that had been a valid comment he had made, she
admitted a little unwillingly. Valid but unfair, she
decided, not giving her a chance to prove herself first.

She did, the next day, have a try at apologising for that
pirouette.

'I'm sorry, Dr Brent,' she said stiffly in the duty
room. 'I shouldn't have been behaving like that.' Adam
Brent didn't look up from the folder in his hand.

'No,' he agreed, 'you shouldn't, Sister Maynard.' He might at least see that this isn't easy for me, Julie thought indignantly.

'Miss Clifford enjoyed it, though,' she said impulsively.

He looked at her. 'Yes, I could see that,' he returned. He put the folder down. 'It would have been somewhat unseemly in any of our staff, Sister,' he said, coolly. 'Do you agree?'

Julie gave up. 'Yes, Dr Brent,' she said, and she hoped that her voice was as cool as his. And that, she thought furiously, is all the apology you'll get out of me, Adam Brent!

She was determined not to let the doctor's attitude spoil her pleasure in her job, and in the lovely old house and her tiny flat under the eaves. There was a swimming pool for the staff and for those of the patients who could use it, and she got into the habit of having a swim whenever she could.

The garden, too, was so big that she hadn't yet explored it all, with wide, shady paths winding under old trees past fragrant frangipani, oleander, hibiscus and bougainvillaea—all bushes she knew and loved from her parents' garden. The paths were wide enough and smooth enough for wheelchairs, and Julie tried to make time to take at least one of her patients out every day.

'I'm going to see that you get out as often as possible, Mr Ramsay,' she told her multiple sclerosis patient one day as she pushed his wheelchair down the ramp from the stoep to the garden. 'Even in winter.'

Ted Ramsay smiled. 'I appreciate the thought, Sister,' he said, 'but I don't think you know what a Cape winter can be like.' Julie looked up at the clear and cloudless blue sky.

'Everyone keeps talking about this Cape winter,' she said, 'but when I look at that sky I just don't believe it.'

'You'll believe it all right, Sister,' the man in the wheelchair assured her, 'when a black south-easter blows and that same sky is dark and stormy.'

'Perhaps,' Julie agreed, and she smiled. 'But right now I can't believe in these Cape storms ahead. Oh, we can't go up this path, I'm afraid, it's too steep. I'll check it out later, and find if there's another way round.'

It was a narrow path, and it led away from the big house. That evening, when she had had her swim, she pulled on her short towelling bath-robe and decided to explore. Perhaps it was only that first part of the path that was steep. It would be nice to find a different way to take someone like Ted Ramsay, who must know all the paths around the house by now.

The path evened out as she turned the corner. And there, ahead of her, was a golden Labrador. He was digging a hole with great enthusiasm, but when he heard her he looked so guilty that Julie burst out laughing.

'I don't know what you're looking for or what you're burying, boy,' she said to him, 'but I'm pretty sure you could be in trouble.'

She knelt down on the path and the dog, seeing that he wasn't to be scolded, came towards her, his tail wagging—slowly at first and then fast. He sat down and offered her a paw, which she gravely shook.

'Do you know,' she said to him, 'I have a very nice girlfriend for you but she's too far away, and I miss her so much.' Just how much, she only realised now with the dog's topaz eyes looking into hers. 'She's called Holly and she isn't pure Labrador, like you, but I don't think you'd mind. You are a handsome fellow, aren't you? I wonder what your name is?'

'It's Shandy,' Adam Brent said behind her.

Julie scrambled to her feet. Did this man always have to see her in embarrassing situations that put her at a disadvantage?

'Oh, is he your dog?' she asked, and she could feel her cheeks aflame. She was very conscious, suddenly, of her short blue beach-robe and her bare brown legs very much in evidence. 'I was just—'

He waited.

'Just making friends with him,' she said, and she thought, which is a lot more than I have a chance of doing with his master! If I wanted to, which I don't.

'Shandy, have you been digging?' the doctor said sternly, looking at the earth on the dog's paws and on his nose.

He looks younger, Julie thought, in a T-shirt and with his hair a bit ruffled. Younger and—not quite as hostile.

'He takes the children's toys and hides them,' he explained. 'I think he's missing them—they'll be back in a few days. I wonder what he was hiding this time?'

Julie showed him the hole Shandy had been working on, and they found a small blue fluffy bear, half-covered with earth.

'Catherine left him here to keep me company,' Adam Brent said, dismayed. 'He's one of her favourites.'

'I'll wash him; he'll be as good as new,' Julie offered impulsively.

'Thank you,' Adam Brent said, and he handed her the toy.

If I don't take this chance to clear the air I'll never do it, Julie thought. She looked up at the doctor.

'Dr Brent,' she said quietly, 'you made up your mind about me without giving me a chance. That isn't fair, you know.'

Adam Brent shrugged. 'I made up my mind on unalterable facts,' he said. 'You can't deny that you're very young, and you can't deny that you have no geriatric experience.'

'I'm old enough to be a qualified sister,' Julie pointed out, managing to keep her voice even. 'And although I

have no geriatric experience, can you fault my care of
my patients?'

Adam Brent's grey eyes rested on her face, and she
forced herself to return his gaze steadily.

'No, I can't do that,' he said at last.

'If you're thinking of—of me dancing for Miss
Clifford, she enjoyed it.'

Julie knew that her voice and the tilt of her chin were
defiant, and she knew, too, that she was probably making
a mistake mentioning this.

'I know that,' Adam Brent said. 'And that's part of
what worries me. That, and Captain O'Connor calling
you Sister Sunshine. They're becoming too fond of you,
and that isn't a good thing.'

'Why not?' Julie asked, taken aback.

'Because they need stability in their lives, these folks
who look on Halvey House as their home now,' the
doctor said quietly. 'It's upsetting for them that they'll
become fond of you and then you'll go.'

'Why should I do that?' Julie said, bewildered.

Adam Brent raised his eyebrows. 'Come on, Sister
Maynard,' he said. 'This isn't the sort of place a girl
like you will be happy in for long.' Slow anger rose
in Julie.

'A girl like me? What do you know, Dr Brent,' she
said, unsteadily, 'of the kind of person I really am? You
haven't given me a chance.'

He looked down at her, his grey eyes dark. Then,
abruptly, he turned and walked away, the dog at
his heels.

I'll show him, Julie thought. I'll make him see just
how wrong he is. It was only when she turned to go
that she realised that she still had the small blue teddy
in her hands.

If I had thought of it in time, she told herself, still
furious, I would have thrown it right after him!

She looked again at the toy, which was obviously well loved—with one ear missing and one leg almost off—no, she couldn't have done that, she thought, when it was obviously precious to a child.

She went up to her room, changed into a cotton dress and put some detergent and warm water in the tiny sink in her bathroom. Then, very carefully, she washed the dirt off the teddy and set him on her window-sill to dry. The next day she sewed his leg on securely, and put a Mickey Mouse plaster—at a jaunty angle—over the place for his missing ear. Then she tied a bright red ribbon round his neck.

She didn't see Adam Brent that day because he was at the Clinic, doing anaesthetics, and she began to think that she had been a little foolish and to wish that she had just washed the toy, put it in a bag and returned it to the doctor. Instead, there Teddy sat on her desk, bright and clean, with his plaster and his jaunty bow.

The next day was one of those days which Julie was coming to know well—the kind of day that could easily run away with her. Miss Clifford's breakfast tray had porridge instead of her usual cereal, Captain O'Connor said his egg was so soft that it was running away and there were teas where there should have been coffees. Julie and Prudence sorted that out and soothed the ruffled feathers of their patients.

No sooner had they done that than the physiotherapist turned up an hour earlier than she was supposed to, very apologetic, because she'd had to make an emergency dentist's appointment for one of her children.

Then the drug cupboard and the linen cupboard had to be checked because, apparently, that was always done in the middle of the month. The patients who could be taken into the sun-room were taken there, and a little later Julie found Miss Clifford and Mrs Smit arguing about whose turn it was to play Scrabble with Captain

O'Connor. Eventually—unwillingly—they agreed they could all three play.

'But it isn't as good with three,' Miss Clifford insisted, surprisingly fiercely.

'Takes two to tango,' hummed the captain—enjoying every bit of this, Julie could see.

She left them to it and went to Ted Ramsay's room. She could see that his physiotherapy treatment had tired him—there was a greyness in his face and lines of pain around his mouth.

'Tough today, Ted?' she asked him. He nodded.

'A little, Sister. But she only did the muscle-stretching exercises today—I told her I'm going home for the weekend, and Dr Brent said I shouldn't tire myself out before I go.'

Ted and his wife and family were all so much looking forward to this weekend, Julie knew. She knew, too, that although Ted was in remission at the moment so many things could change this; could cause the multiple sclerosis to become active again. A cold, a minor infection, stress, fatigue. And yet it was so important to do everything possible to combat the progressive muscle dysfunction which was part of the disease.

'Rest now, Ted,' she told him, and eased another pillow behind him. 'Save your energy for the weekend.' She picked up a picture of a laughing baby in the arms of a pretty dark-haired girl. 'You must be looking forward to seeing your little granddaughter—they're coming from East London for the weekend, I believe?'

When she could see that he was comfortable, and giving her a smile in return—and he is one, she thought, who never complains, no matter how bad he feels—she went back to her office.

At the door, she stopped. Adam Brent was standing there, and he was holding the blue teddy in his hands.

'Dr Brent,' Julie said, uncertainly. The doctor turned round.

'Did you do this?' he asked her. Gently, awkwardly, his big brown hands touched the mended leg, the Mickey Mouse plaster, the jaunty red bow. Julie nodded, all at once at a loss for words.

'I don't know what to say.' Adam Brent's grey eyes met hers, and for the first time since she had met him there was no coolness, no hostility.

CHAPTER TWO

IN THAT moment, Julie thought afterwards, so many things changed between Adam Brent and her.

She could see that he was finding it difficult to equate the young woman he was so sure he had identified with someone who could mend a little girl's toy—and tie a ribbon round its neck.

For her part, she knew that she was seeing beyond the cool hostility Adam Brent had shown her to a man who was touched by the unexpectedness of what she had done.

'Thank you, Sister Maynard,' the doctor said at last awkwardly. 'This was—very kind of you. I know Catherine will be so pleased.'

Julie could see that it hadn't been easy for him to say this, or to accept that she had done something which upset his preconceived idea of—what had he said? 'A girl like you.'

She was glad, then and afterwards, that she managed to lighten the moment by saying to him that it might be a good idea to keep the blue teddy well out of the dog's reach.

'I'll certainly do that,' Adam replied. He hesitated and then, still a little awkward, he said, 'You were telling Shandy about Holly? Is she your dog?'

'Our family dog,' Julie told him. 'She's mostly Labrador, and not too clever, but we all love her dearly.'

'A dog of little brain?' Adam suggested, and she realised that he was within an ace of smiling.

'Oh, yes,' Julie agreed, and she couldn't help smiling in return.

Another surprise, she thought, although he would surely have met Winnie-the-Pooh through his children.

There were still times, in the following days, when she could see that he hadn't forgotten his reservations about her—she could see that in the way he looked at her. But, somehow, the initial hostility she had been so well aware of had become a guarded acceptance that she seemed to be doing her job pretty well.

It would be nice, she found herself thinking once— and surprised herself at the thought—if he could be as casually friendly with her as he was with Brenda Morkel, who was Sister on the first floor. But then she would remind herself that Adam and Brenda had trained together and that their children went to the same nursery school.

And, in any case, she could live without Adam Brent's friendship, she would tell herself. She didn't even have to see him that often, so it wasn't any big deal.

Matron agreed with no difficulty to Mrs Ngalo's smaller grandchildren being brought in to visit her, and Julie could see that even the thought of this had made life brighter for her hip-replacement patient.

The afternoon that two of her daughters were due to bring their children Julie and Prudence got her up and into a wheelchair. 'You're to promise to ring for us if you're tired, Mrs Ngalo,' Julie said, more than a little concerned. 'They can just as well have their visit with you in bed.'

'The little ones will be worried to see their grandmother in bed,' Mrs Ngalo said firmly. 'But, yes, Sister, I will not be foolish, and I will ring for you if I do need to be back in bed.'

So when the bell did ring from Room Six Julie, on duty alone while Prudence was at tea, hurried along— to find her patient looking better than she had ever seen her, with one dark-eyed baby on her lap and a toddler clinging to her knees.

'Sister,' Mrs Ngalo said proudly, 'this is Sipho, and the little girl is Lindiwe. And, thank you, perhaps I should be back in bed now.'

Julie helped her back into bed, settled her comfortably and then, because the ward was always quiet at visiting time—and, in any case, she could hear any other bell—couldn't resist these two adorable children. The little girl, Lindiwe, was prepared to come to her, although the baby, Sipho, clung to his pretty young mother, happier just to peep at her with a shy smile.

'How old is she?' she asked, as the toddler came towards her outstretched arms, a little unsteady on her chubby little legs.

'Eighteen months,' her mother said.

Just then Lindiwe reached Julie, not at all uncomfortable with the stranger who picked her up and hugged her.

'Oh, Dr Brent,' Mrs Ngalo said, 'you did come to see my grandchildren.'

'Couldn't miss it once you told me they were coming,' Adam Brent said. 'Obviously, neither could Sister Maynard.'

Julie felt her cheeks grow warm and she set little Lindiwe down carefully, trying without much success to straighten the strands of hair that the little girl had pulled loose.

Back in her office, she was just pinning up a blonde curl when Adam Brent came in.

'That was a good idea, Sister,' he said. 'Mrs Ngalo looks so much brighter.'

'It wasn't difficult,' Julie told him honestly. 'Matron said of course they could come; she would have said the same to anyone who asked.'

'Yes, but you were the one who thought of asking,' the doctor said. He smiled, and it was a smile with no reserve in it. 'I think, though, you've really started something. Nurse Solomon just came in, on her way back from tea, and she's claimed both the little ones. She's taking them in to see the other patients.'

Julie hesitated, but only for a moment.

'I think it will do them all the world of good,' she said. 'Halvey House is so good in so many ways—for the long-term patients, everyone really does so much to help them to feel this is a home from home. But they are all old folks, and I'm sure they miss contact with children. And with animals.'

It was only now, as she was talking, that she thought of something.

'Couldn't you bring Shandy in to see them?' she asked eagerly. 'I know Mrs Smit misses her dogs from the farm—she and I often talk about dogs—and Ted Ramsay has been telling me about his collie. It would be great for them to have a visit from Shandy.'

'I suppose I could,' Adam Brent said after a moment. And then he added, 'Maybe we could start off by bringing him to the garden, or to the stoep, to visit the folks who are outside. I don't know what Matron would say if we start bringing dogs right into the wards.'

Julie didn't think Matron would object. Most matrons would, she knew, but Mrs Carstens seemed to be willing and able to bend rules and to be much more flexible than any matron Julie had ever known. The right kind of person for Halvey House, she found herself thinking more and more.

Just as Adam Brent was the right kind of doctor. All the patients liked him, and they trusted him. He was never too busy to stop and spend time with each one. Julie felt more than a little ashamed when she remembered that she had said to him that she looked on her patients as people first, their age being irrelevant— the inference being, she was all too aware, that perhaps

he didn't. But he certainly looked on his patients as
people first and foremost, and she had come to see that
he was right—she had been naïve in thinking that age
was irrelevant.

Something else she began to realise was that although
he had come to accept her on a professional level he
didn't want to go any further than that in terms of being
friendly when he made his visits to the floor she was in
charge of. Thus far, and no further was the message that
came over very clearly.

And that was fine by her, she assured herself. Not
that a little more warmth and friendliness would go
amiss. It was only romantic entanglements she was
determined to keep very clear of and there was certainly
no danger of that, either from Adam Brent's side or
from hers, because he wasn't her type at all.

Sometimes—not often, but sometimes—on warm
summer evenings when she looked up at Table Mountain, floodlit for summer, she would find herself
remembering other warm evenings when she hadn't
been alone. Tim Curran, the doctor who had taken her
to that Hospital Ball, with his dark, laughing eyes and
the cleft in his chin. Mark Elliott, tall and dark and so
full of charm that any girl with any sense would have
known not to be taken in by that charm.

They are both history, Julie told herself severely. My
life is just the way I want it to be—quiet, pleasant and
unstressed.

Ted Ramsay, her multiple sclerosis patient, was well
enough to go home for the weekend, although there
were a few moments on the Friday when Julie wondered
if it was wise.

'I'm worried about him,' she admitted to Adam Brent
just before the hospital Kombi left to take Ted and
his wheelchair home. 'I know he's in remission at the
moment, and there's nothing I can put my finger on.

His temperature is normal, there's no sign of any deterioration in his coordination and he didn't look as tired after his physio. But—'

She hesitated.

'It's just a feeling you have?' Adam Brent suggested, and she nodded, relieved that he wasn't brushing what seemed to be groundless concerns aside.

'I think he may be coming to a flare-up again,' she said slowly.

The doctor's grey eyes met hers.

'You may be right,' he agreed, 'but I don't think his visit home will precipitate that. And, if he is heading for a flare-up, this could well be his last chance of a visit home for some time.' Unexpectedly he smiled. 'But I know what you mean about that sort of feeling. I've had it too. You can't justify it medically but I've learned that that doesn't matter—it can be pretty valid. Anyway, Sister Maynard, I think the best thing we can do is let Ted have his weekend at home, and enjoy it.'

He looked at his watch. 'I have to be at the Clinic to do an anaesthetic for Dr Morrison. There's just time to see Ted on his way.'

They went along the corridor and met Prudence coming out of Ted Ramsay's room, pushing the wheel-chair. Ted's thin face was alight and, not for the first time, Julie's heart ached for this man who was just over sixty, but who knew—and had accepted—that he would never be well enough to go home for any length of time.

'Have a nice weekend, Ted,' she said as they pushed the wheelchair up the ramp and into the Kombi. 'And tell me all about little Natasha—she looks such a poppet.'

'Bye, Tom,' Adam Brent said. 'Goodbye, Sister Maynard.'

He walked over to his own car, reversed out and headed down towards the city and the Clinic. Julie had a fleeting picture of him gowned and masked for

Theatre, and she found herself thinking that she would
enjoy doing that sort of work with him.

With Ted Ramsay away, and most of the other occupants of her floor having visitors, Julie's working
weekend was fairly quiet. Neither Captain O'Connor
nor Miss Clifford had visitors, and when she looked in
the captain was asleep, sitting in his wheelchair and
snoring gently. Julie eased his head into a more comfortable position, with a small pillow behind it, and then
she went into Miss Clifford's room.

'I thought I'd have tea with you, Miss Clifford,' she
said. 'Everything's quiet, and I'll hear the bell if anyone
does want me.'

Miss Clifford's face lit up.

'How nice of you, my dear,' she said. 'I was just
sitting looking out the window at the city hall—look,
you can just see the roof down there—and remembering
when I danced Giselle there.' She shook her silvery head
and smiled. 'You should have seen the bouquets I got
at the end—I always did and, do you know, there was
always a bunch of deep red roses every time I danced.'

'From someone special?' Julie asked, setting Miss
Clifford's cup where her swollen hands could reach it
easily. The old lady blushed.

'Well, my dear, I never knew who it was but I had
my suspicions. The first violinist in the city orchestra—
he was Polish, and he was so romantic. But of course
my career came first.'

'What was your favourite role?' Julie asked. The silvery head tilted to one side.

'The critics liked my Juliet,' she said thoughtfully,
'but I think I enjoyed *Swan Lake* best of all. Of course,
if I had accepted the offer to go to Covent Garden—'

'But you didn't,' Julie prompted as the old lady went
silent. It wasn't the first time she had heard the story,

by any means, but she knew how much pleasure it gave Miss Clifford to tell it.

'No, I felt that I could do more for ballet by dancing right here in Cape Town. But I do sometimes wonder how different my life would have been if I had gone to Covent Garden.'

A bell rang, and Julie stood up.

'Sounds as if it's Captain O'Connor,' she said. 'Sorry, Miss Clifford, but I'll have to go.'

'You could bring him along to see me,' Miss Clifford suggested. 'I know Mrs Smit has visitors today, and the captain and I could keep each other company.'

'I'll see what he says,' Julie promised, and as she went along to Captain O'Connor's room she was smiling. Mrs Smit and Miss Clifford vied for the old man's attention, and he loved it.

'Where's my tea?' the captain demanded when she went in. 'Sure and it's way past teatime, and me poor old throat that parched.'

'I didn't want your tea to get cold—I'll bring you some now,' Julie said.

'Asleep, was I?' he asked when she went back with tea for him.

'Well, your eyes were closed, and I didn't want to disturb you,' Julie said. 'Especially when Sister Wilson said you didn't have a very good night.'

'Couldn't get myself comfortable somehow,' the old man said. 'But I feel the better for the snooze, I must say.'

'Miss Clifford is wondering if you would like to visit her,' Julie said.

'If I do she'll be after telling Mrs Smit the minute she sees her,' Captain O'Connor said, and he smiled like a naughty schoolboy.

'She's been telling me about her dancing,' Julie said.

'Has she now? That would be the stories of her

dancing Giselle, and the red roses from her secret admirer in the orchestra?' He shook his head. 'Well, now,' he said, 'it can't be doing anyone any harm, now can it?'

Julie looked at him. 'I must say I was wondering—'

'All in her head,' he told her cheerfully. 'I think maybe she was in the—what do you call it—the line-up.'

'The *corps de ballet*?' Julie said, and he nodded.

'And then she left, and she taught ballet to the little children in the townships—and sure and is that not every bit as worth while as stories of dancing at Covent Garden?' At Julie's look of enquiry he went on. 'It was one of her visitors told me that, and made me promise I would never let Miss Clifford know that she told me.'

His bushy white eyebrows drew together fiercely. 'And I know you will not be letting on either, Sister.'

'No, I won't,' Julie assured him, touched not only by what he had told her but by his own determination to let Miss Clifford have her dreams.

There was a message on her desk when she went back to her office to tell her that the night sister, Sister Anderson, had flu and an agency sister would be taking over.

The agency sister was about Julie's age, but she admitted that this would be her first time in complete charge of a floor and she was nervous.

'I'm in a flat here in the house,' Julie told her. 'Here's my telephone number—ring me if you need me.'

She did it to give the agency sister confidence, but when her telephone rang and she heard the agency sister's anxious voice she was very glad that she had.

'Sister Maynard? It's Mr Carter in Five. He's dizzy and nauseous, and he has a sharp pain in his left arm.'

'Have you let Dr Brent know?' Julie asked, pulling on jeans and a T-shirt as she spoke.

'Not yet—I thought I should speak to you first.'

'I'll be right down,' Julie said.

Mr Carter. He was another stroke patient, but this sounded like myocardial infarction.

'Send for Dr Brent,' she said tersely as soon as she saw the old man. His skin was grey and clammy, and his pulse rapid and irregular. 'His number is beside the phone. Tell him I think it's MI.'

It was only a few minutes before Adam Brent arrived, his brown hair rumpled and his clothes hastily pulled on.

'He's in shock,' he said, looking at Julie. 'I want to get him to the cardiac care unit at the Clinic, but we'll have to stabilise him before he can be moved. I'll phone them right away. I want his blood pressure, Sister.'

He strode out of the room and along the corridor, and Julie prepared to take the old man's blood pressure.

'Eighty over thirty, Dr Brent,' she said when Adam came back.

'Too low. We'll set up an intravenous infusion, and see how he does,' Adam said.

It was the first time that they had worked together as a team but Julie found that she could anticipate what the doctor wanted, her hands steady as she kept the infusion tubing at the best angle to prevent air from entering the vein.

'I think he'll do,' Adam said tiredly at last, and soon after that the ambulance arrived from the Clinic. Quietly and efficiently the paramedics lifted the old man onto a stretcher, the intravenous infusion carefully in place. Adam and Julie went down in the lift as well, and in the darkened hall Adam looked at Julie.

'I'll take my car and go down to the Clinic too.'

'Will you let me know how he does?' Julie asked him. 'I'll wait outside on the stoep.'

'You're tired,' he said unexpectedly. 'You should go to bed.'

She shook her head. 'I wouldn't be able to sleep,' she told him.

It was a warm, still night and she sat down on one of the wicker couches on the stoep, wondering how long Adam would be. It was just after one—she couldn't remember when her phone had rung, but it must have been about midnight.

She meant just to sit there, waiting, but slowly weariness crept over her and, in spite of her certainty that she wouldn't be able to sleep, she closed her eyes. And woke with a start, to see Adam Brent beside her.

'How is he?' she asked, instantly awake.

'He's going to be all right,' the doctor said, sitting down beside her and leaning back. 'They'll keep him at the Clinic for a few days, but he should be back here Thursday or Friday.'

'That poor agency sister,' Julie said feelingly. 'Something like this happening on her first night in charge. I'm glad I left her my phone number; she would—'

She stopped. Adam Brent's eyes were closed. She remembered then that he had been at the Clinic for a good part of the day, and then this crisis. No wonder he was tired.

He looked different asleep, she thought. Younger, more vulnerable. She wondered what she should do. Perhaps it would be better to leave him here, on the darkened stoep, asleep. She knew, from Brenda Morkel, that his children were still with their grandparents so it wouldn't matter if he didn't go back to the cottage for a bit.

Gently she leaned over to move the cushion so that he wouldn't wake up with a stiff neck but, as she did, he opened his eyes.

I should have moved back right away, Julie thought afterwards. But she didn't.

He was very close to her in the warm darkness. Too

close, she thought, and she could feel her heart thudding unevenly.

'Sister Sunshine,' he murmured sleepily.

And then, very softly, for the first time he said her name.

'Julie.'

CHAPTER THREE

PERHAPS it was her own uneven heartbeat Julie could feel; perhaps it was Adam's. He was so close to her that one movement—one small movement—and she would be in his arms. And there was nothing she could do, nothing she wanted to do, in that endless moment to stop that.

It was Adam who moved away.

'I'm sorry, Sister Maynard,' he said, his voice stiff, formal. 'I was half-asleep—I must be more tired than I thought.'

Or I wouldn't have come close to kissing you. The words were unspoken, but she knew very well that that was what he was thinking.

'Thanks for coming in when you weren't on duty,' Adam Brent said. 'Lucky you were in—Saturday night and all.'

Julie stood up.

'Yes,' she said lightly, knowing her voice sounded brittle, 'lucky I was in on Saturday night, a girl like me, Dr Brent.'

She thought he made a movement—of denial or of protest—when she said that, but she didn't want to find out. Without looking at him, she went inside and closed the big front door behind her. Ignoring the lift, she ran up the three flights of stairs, stopping only when, breathless, she had closed her own door behind her.

And now the stab of hurt was replaced by anger. Anger at Adam Brent and, even more, anger at herself for that moment when she had wanted him to take her in his arms—to hold her, to kiss her.

And how can that be when I don't even like the man? she wondered, bewildered and shaken. Lucky she'd been in, indeed. She hadn't been out once on a date, which was obviously what he'd meant, on a Saturday night or any other since she started work here.

'Then it's time you were,' her friend Meg said on the phone the next night.

Somehow, although Julie had phoned Meg to let off steam about Adam Brent, she hadn't said a word about him. Only said that work was fine. But Meg had been right; maybe she did need to remember those other pebbles on the beach.

'Not that it bothers me,' she said hastily when Meg said briskly that it was time she did. With some difficulty Julie laughed. 'Anyway, I don't know any pebbles here in Cape Town.'

'Listen, Julie,' Meg said after a moment, 'there's a long weekend coming up—Monday holiday—and some of us were wondering what to do. We thought about a beach weekend, or maybe the casino at the Wild Coast, but I'm thinking now why don't we come to Cape Town for the weekend?'

'Oh, Meg, it's much too far,' Julie protested, torn between delight and dismay.

'Oh, we wouldn't drive,' Meg said airily. 'We'd get one of those cheap middle-of-the-night flights. Look, I'll let you know but it sounds like fun.'

I suppose it does, Julie thought doubtfully as she put the phone down—Meg, and some of their friends from the hospital. Yes, she told herself determinedly, it does sound like fun. And, perhaps, just what I need. Maybe if I went out dancing, had a light-hearted kiss or two on a beach in the moonlight, I might not be so ready to fall into Adam Brent's arms!

Not that she had, she reminded herself. Only wanted to.

She hadn't seen him that day, and she was grateful for that. Sometimes he did look in on Sundays, even although he was officially off, but perhaps he had chosen not to after last night.

And, fortunately, Monday was always busy, so when he did come Julie was downstairs with Matron, leaving Prudence in charge of the wards. The doctor was just leaving as she got back.

'Ah, Sister Maynard,' he said, his voice as formal as always—not that she had expected anything different. 'I've just been in to see Ted Ramsay—he looks none the worse for his weekend at home.'

'Better, I would say,' Julie replied just as formally. 'I think it did him a lot of good.'

'Yes, I would agree,' Adam Brent returned. They were standing outside her office and he looked down at her, his grey eyes all at once darker. 'Sister Maynard,' he began, and then he stopped.

Julie found herself back in that moment in the warm darkness of the stoep. Unaccountably her heart lurched.

'Yes, Dr Brent?' she said.

'I phoned the Clinic this morning,' he said. 'Old Bob Carter is doing nicely. He's out of Cardiac Intensive Care, and they're very happy with his progress.'

Julie was certain that that wasn't what he had intended saying.

'I'm glad to hear that,' she replied. 'They'll let us know when he can come back?' Abruptly he nodded, and walked away.

Julie went back to work, glad of the busy day and the challenge of keeping her floor running smoothly—sorting out problems, keeping her old folks happy.

Miss Clifford's hands were even more swollen because the weather had been so hot, and Julie debated with herself the question of whether increasing her medication would help or whether the possible side-effects were too unpleasant. She made a note to discuss that with Adam Brent.

Mrs Smit lacked co-operation with the physiotherapist, in spite of Julie and the physiotherapist pointing out that there could be no question of her getting home until she was more mobile. There had also been a little spat between Mrs Smit and Miss Clifford when they both went to visit Captain O'Connor at the same time.

She was just coming off duty the following evening when the porter phoned to say that there was someone to see her in the hall. Julie had already handed over, so she said she would be down in five minutes.

When she got out of the lift the porter smiled, and told her that her visitors were on the stoep.

Julie went outside, puzzled to have visitors and even more puzzled by the porter's amusement.

But she understood when she went outside. The big golden dog, Shandy, was sitting at the top of the steps. A small girl held his lead, and her brown hair and grey eyes told Julie that this was Adam's daughter. An even smaller boy, with copper hair and blue eyes and freckles, had a firm grasp of Shandy's collar.

Recognising Julie, the dog started to come to her. 'Sit, Shandy,' the little girl said sternly, but the dog pulled her towards Julie. 'He's usually very good,' she said anxiously, 'but I think he's pleased to see you.'

'I think he is,' Julie agreed, and she bent down to accept the paw Shandy was offering her.

'I'm Catherine, and this is my brother David,' the child said.

'Hello, Catherine,' Julie replied. Because Catherine seemed uncertain what to do next, she said, 'Did you come to see me?'

Catherine nodded.

'We wanted to thank you for making Blue Ted so nice,' she said. 'We got back from Granny and Grandad

today, and I was so worried all the time about Blue Ted
cos I forgot him and I thought he would be so lonely
and so sad. And then I saw him, and I was so happy.'

'Catherine thought it was the fairies what done it,'
the little boy volunteered. 'With magic.' His sister
turned to him.

'I did not,' she said fiercely, and all too obviously
untruthfully. She looked up at Julie. 'Daddy said he
would bring us to see you so that I could say thank you,
but he had to go to the Clinic for a 'mergency so David
and me thought we'd just come. Cos I wanted to thank
you right away.'

'It was a pleasure,' Julie assured her. 'I really enjoyed
washing your teddy and making him smart again.'

'It was very naughty of Shandy,' the little boy said
earnestly. 'But Daddy thinks it was cos he was lonely
for us.'

The big dog wagged his tail a little anxiously, remembering, it seemed, that he had been in trouble.

'We'll have to go now,' Catherine said. 'Daddy asked
Beauty to stay with us until he came back, and we said
we wouldn't be long.'

'I'll walk back with you,' Julie offered, and the two
small faces—Catherine's serious, David's somehow
impish—lit up. They walked past the swimming pool,
and up the path to the doctor's cottage.

'Daddy told us you have a dog called Holly,' David
said. 'Could you bring her to visit Shandy?'

Julie had a moment's surprise that Adam Brent had
remembered what she had said, and that he had told his
children.

'I wish I could, David,' Julie said, meaning it. 'But
Holly lives with my mum and dad in Durban, and that's
a long way away.'

'We once went to Durban for a holiday—to a place
called Chaka's Rock. That was before Mummy died,'

Catherine said, and her matter-of-fact little voice brought an unexpected ache to Julie's heart.

At the top of the path a very large woman was waiting.

'You didn't tell me you were taking that dog with you, Catherine,' she said sternly. 'And it's time for David's bath.'

'Shandy was very good, wasn't he?' Catherine said quickly.

'He certainly was good,' Julie put in. 'He was no trouble at all.'

'What's your name?' David asked, his copper head tilted to one side.

'David, that's rude,' Catherine told him.

'No, you just want to know what to call me, don't you, David?' Julie said. 'It's Julie.'

'Julie,' David repeated, trying it out. 'It's a nice name. It's like June, only Julie.'

'Would you like to come and see my room, Julie?' Catherine asked. 'You can see the special place where Blue Ted sits on my bed.'

'Some other time, thank you, Catherine,' Julie replied, and she thought—not without an invitation from your father! And then, realising that she didn't know when Adam Brent would be back, she said, 'I'll have to go now, but I've so much enjoyed meeting you. Perhaps—'

'Here's Daddy; he's home,' David said joyfully, and he ran to meet the blue estate car which had just drawn up.

Julie's heart sank.

Adam Brent, just out of the car, caught the little boy and lifted him high in the air. Catherine, more sedate but just as eager, went over to him too and he took her hand. The big golden dog jumped up and down beside them, wanting his share of attention as well.

'I'm sorry, kids,' Adam Brent said. 'It's probably too

late for me to take you to see Sister Maynard now, but
we'll go tomorrow.'

'She's here, Daddy. Julie's here,' David told him
excitedly. He hadn't seen her, Julie realised, because
she was under the big oak tree.

'We went to see her at the big house, Daddy,'
Catherine said quickly. 'But we didn't disturb her; we
waited until she would be coming off duty.'

'And it was a lovely surprise for me,' Julie said
quickly, as the doctor frowned. And then, daring him
to reprimand the children, she said, 'It was so nice of
Catherine to want to thank me right away.'

'And I want to show Julie my room, and Blue Ted's
cushion, and all my dolls, and—'

'Catherine, I'd love to see all your precious things,
but perhaps some other time,' Julie said quickly before
Adam could say anything. 'I have to go back now and
change out of my uniform and have supper.'

For a moment Adam's grey eyes met hers, then he
looked down at his small daughter.

'As Sister Maynard says, perhaps some other time,'
he said evenly. 'Thank you for bringing them back,
Sister. David, I see I'm in time to bath you so we can
let Beauty get off home now.'

'You can't say "Sister Maynard", Daddy, not when
we can call her Julie,' Catherine said earnestly. The
doctor, to Julie's amusement, avoided that one by pretending that he hadn't heard.

'Has Shandy had his supper yet?' he asked briskly.
Julie thought it could help to rescue him.

'Bye, Catherine,' she said. 'Bye, David.'

Just before she turned the corner, she looked back.
Adam Brent was walking into the cottage, with a child
holding each hand and the dog beside them. For a
moment he wasn't the remote, sometimes hostile, so
recently disturbing doctor. He was just a man with two

small children—a man who should have had his wife waiting for him inside the small thatched cottage.

And, as Julie walked back to the big house, she found herself thinking that Adam Brent's life must be far from easy. And it must be lonely.

Meg phoned the following night to say that she and Ryan and Nick were flying down on Thursday night.

'Well, Friday morning, actually,' she said blithely. 'We arrive at some unearthly hour—four o'clock, I think. Ryan and Nick will both be exhausted. Ryan's still on Casualty, and Nick's just finished with his babies—did his final delivery last night.'

'What about you?' Julie asked, her spirits lifting at the thought of seeing Meg and the two young interns. 'You're still in Theatre, aren't you?'

'Yes, but our list has been quite civilised—don't worry, I'll have lots of energy for painting Cape Town red,' Meg assured her. 'And thanks, but you don't have to meet us. Ryan has a cousin who lives in Camps Bay. We're going to stay with him; he'll meet us.'

They made arrangements for Friday evening as Julie would be off duty for the weekend.

'We'll have fun,' Meg said happily.

It was even fun, Julie realised with surprise, getting ready to go out—hurrying to shower and change, to wash her hair and dry it quickly, to choose between the kingfisher-blue dress with the shoestring straps and the white one with the scoop neckline. The blue dress, she decided, and she would just leave her hair loose; it had dried nice and curly.

Ryan's cousin, it turned out, not only had a cottage almost on the beach at Camps Bay he had a beach buggy, and Meg and the two young doctors arrived in that. There were hugs and kisses when Julie ran down the steps to meet them and they were off, heading down towards the city—its lights twinkling like a carpet of stars.

'Where are we going?' Julie asked.

'To the Waterfront complex at the harbour,' Ryan told her. 'Everyone says it's where the action is—my cousin told us about a great place for jazz, and there's a place with Creole food, and we can dance too.'

Julie hadn't been to the Waterfront, and that Friday night it seemed to have a holiday atmosphere. They listened to jazz, they ate at the Creole restaurant, they danced and they walked past the moored cruise ships right to the sea.

'If we're lucky we might see seals—the moonlight's bright enough,' Nick said, his arm casually round Julie's waist. 'Pity the Penny Ferry doesn't sail at night.'

The Penny Ferry, he told them, used to cost just that, moving people from one part of what used to be the docks to another.

'Costs a heck of a lot more than that now,' he said, 'but you get even closer to the seals.'

They thought that they saw sleek, dark heads bobbing against the pier but even with the bright moonlight, it was difficult to be sure.

'We could do with something like this in Durban,' Meg commented. She looked at Julie. 'I could go for living in Cape Town, you know, Julie, with places like this to come to. What else should we do? We're tourists and holiday-makers, remember. What do Cape Town people do for fun—besides the Waterfront, I mean?'

Julie thought about that.

'I'm not sure,' she admitted. 'Most of the folks I work with lead pretty quiet lives—they work, and they go home. Actually, the only young one is Prudence and she's engaged; they're saving like mad, so they don't go out much. I think people go to the beach, or they walk on the mountain. Oh, and, of course, there's the Wine Route—we should certainly do that.'

They were back at the bright and busy part of the Waterfront now. 'But it looks to me,' she said, 'as if a lot of Cape Town folks come here; this crowd can't be all people on holiday.'

'But the people you work with don't come to the Waterfront in the evenings?' Ryan asked.

'I shouldn't think so,' Julie replied, and she had a sudden slightly disquieting memory of Adam Brent going into his house with his children and his dog.

They had coffee and they discussed going on the Wine Route the next day, then the others took Julie back to Halvey House.

'I'm not usually a fader,' Ryan said, yawning, 'but that middle-of-the-night flight was a bit much for me.'

'Not to mention my bonus twins on Wednesday night,' Nick said. 'Ever delivered twins, Julie, in your midder days? I tell you, if you think delivering one baby is a thrill you don't know what it's like with two.'

Ryan drew up outside the big house, dark except for one or two lights on each floor. He jumped out, and helped Julie down.

'We miss you, you know, Julie, love,' he told her earnestly. 'The hospital isn't the same without you; the parties aren't the same; the—'

'Come on, Ryan, Nick's asleep and I'm exhausted,' Meg said plaintively. 'Save the rest for tomorrow.'

The young fair-haired doctor sighed. 'I could give you the keys,' he suggested. 'Then you and Nick could to back to Camps Bay, and I could go up to Julie's flat with her and seduce her. Wouldn't that be a good idea, Julie?' Julie laughed.

'I don't think so, Ryan,' she said. 'For one thing, I don't think gentleman visitors are encouraged here and, for another, I don't think I really feel like being seduced tonight, thank you. Can I take a rain-check on it? And, for goodness' sake, keep your voice down. Remember there are people sleeping.' Ryan put his hand over his heart.

'If that's how you feel, I guess I'll have to settle for the rain-check,' he said. 'Goodnight, love of my life.'

'One of the loves of your life,' Julie corrected him, smiling. He took her in his arms then, and kissed her with great enthusiasm. Julie stood on the steps and waved as they drove off, but as she turned a figure rose from one of the chairs.

'I gather you had a pleasant evening, Sister Maynard?' Adam Brent said.

How long had he been there?

All the time, of course, Julie realised with dismay. He must have heard the foolish exchange; he must have seen Ryan kiss her and, being Adam Brent, he would surely have taken the light-hearted exchange seriously. And then, crowding out her concern about this, she realised something else.

'What are you doing here?' she asked him, forgetting to be polite. 'Who needed you at this time of night?'

'At two o'clock in the morning, you mean?' the doctor said. 'Not one of your patients, Sister Maynard. It was Mrs Johnson on the first floor. She has emphysema, and she had a viral infection. You know how suddenly the breathing can deteriorate. But she's stabilised on a bronchodilator.'

His voice was brusque. 'I was just coming out when I heard you and your friends arrive. I didn't want to—disturb you,' he said.

Julie lifted her chin, about to explain that Meg, Nick and Ryan were friends from the hospital in Durban and that they had all known each other since their training days. But she stopped herself. Why should I? she thought, indignant now.

'Thank you for that consideration, Dr Brent,' she said coolly. 'Goodnight.' He didn't stand aside to allow her to pass.

'You are very free with your kisses,' he said, and his voice wasn't quite steady.

'Free with my kisses?' Julie repeated, taken aback.

'That's what I said,' Adam Brent said, evenly now. 'And if that's so—'

His hands were on her arms, stopping her from pushing past him. Once again she could feel the uneven throbbing of her heart. He drew her closer to him and put his arms around her. And then, in the warm darkness, his lips found hers.

His kiss was urgent, demanding, and, after a moment's resistance, there was nothing she could do to stop her body's response to him. There was no room for any concern about anyone coming; no room for anything but this man, his arms around her and his lips on hers so fiercely.

And then, slowly, the fierce urgency was gone, and he was kissing her in a different way. Slow—warm—

Suddenly, abruptly, he let her go.

For a long, endless time she was conscious of him looking down at her, although she could hardly see him. Then, without a word, he turned and walked away—down the steps, away from the big house, into the darkness.

Slowly Julie went up to her room. She was rubbing her arm, she realised, where his fingers had dug into her.

Inside her room, she looked at herself in the mirror. Her hair was untidy, the fair curls tousled on her forehead and her shoulders. Brown eyes looked back at her questioningly. Her cheeks were flushed and one of her blue shoestring straps had slipped down, leaving her brown shoulder bare.

Why did he do that, she thought, bewildered and

shaken. And why did I let him? The answers weren't
too hard. He kissed me because he wanted to, she
thought. And I let him because I wanted him to. She
sat down on her bed.

It was more than just letting him kiss her, she thought
slowly and honestly. She had responded; she had kissed
him back just as fiercely as he had kissed her. She
could remember, now, her arms around him, holding
him close to her.

Slow, warm colour flooded her cheeks. How in all
the world was she to face Adam Brent in the ward on
Monday? Oh, it wasn't the first time she had been kissed
by a doctor she worked with—not by a long chalk—
but no other kiss, in all her life, had been quite like that.

It was a long time before she fell asleep and, when
she did, her dreams were disturbed and confused, a mix-
ture of reality and impossibility. Adam Brent holding
out a single rose to her and then, when she was about
to take it, throwing it down on the ground. Ryan, laughing as he took her arm and led her away from a man
with his back to them—a man Julie knew was Adam
Brent. Mark Elliott, out of her life for six months now,
explaining to her—very reasonably—why he hadn't
told her that he was engaged. Captain O'Connor, telling
her that the doctor was a lonely man, mavourneen.

She was glad, in the morning, that there were still
two days before she would have to see the doctor again;
glad of the light-hearted company of her friends to take
her mind off the question of how Adam Brent would
behave; how she would behave; what he would say and
what she would say.

They went on the Wine Route, driving out to
Stellenbosch through the beautiful, vine-rich countryside
and stopping at different wine farms. They had a cheese
lunch at Lanzerac because Meg insisted on seeing the
old Cape Dutch homestead, now a hotel.

In the evening Ryan's cousin had a braai and this, it turned out, was what Meg had asked him to do so that Julie could meet some Cape Town people.

'Cape Town people?' Julie repeated suspiciously. Meg shrugged.

'All right,' she admitted, 'Cape Town men. Look, nice as it is to have this weekend, it's just a weekend; you need something ongoing, and we're too far away. So—' Julie didn't know whether to be amused or annoyed.

'What on earth did you tell Ryan's cousin?' she said. 'That I'm a poor, lonely nurse who needs her friends to help her to meet people?'

Meg shook her head. 'I didn't need to do that,' she said reasonably. 'I just told him you didn't have much chance to meet people, working in an old-age hospital, and he said he wasn't surprised and, well, he liked the idea of having a braai, anyway.'

It was fun, Julie found, in spite of her misgivings, and she did meet quite a few people, exchanging telephone numbers. She knew that the young accountant would phone her, and she was pretty sure that the computer man and the car salesman would get in touch with her as well. Ryan's cousin and his girlfriend, both in advertising, were fun too, and she could see they meant it when they told her to give them a ring and come back to see them.

But when the evening was over and she was alone, she was shaken to realise that she wasn't thinking about anyone she had met that night—she was thinking about Adam Brent, and the way she had felt when he'd kissed her.

The next day determinedly she put him out of her mind, and set out to make the most of this last day with her friends.

They drove to Cape Point to look at the place where

two oceans met, and Nick took photos of a troop of baboons who were a little too interested in their car.

'Not any closer, Nick,' Meg said nervously. 'Look at all the notices, telling you not to feed the baboons.'

'I'm not feeding them,' Nick pointed out. 'I just want a close-up of that mother with her baby.'

'You know you're not feeding them, but do they?' Meg asked, and certainly the biggest baboon almost seemed to be shaking his fist at them. They got back into the beach buggy, all too aware that it was an open vehicle.

'We'll have to come back. There's too much we haven't had time to do,' Meg said that evening when they dropped Julie back at Halvey House.

'You do have tomorrow,' Julie pointed out, 'since your flight is only at one in the morning. What do you think you'll do?'

'Sandy Bay,' Nick and Ryan said together.

'I haven't said yes to that yet,' Meg said hastily, and Julie laughed as Sandy Bay was a nudist beach.

It was time to say goodbye then, and Julie couldn't help having a quick glance at the stoep just to make sure there was no one there. When the two young doctors were back in the car Meg hugged Julie.

'We haven't had time for a good talk,' she said. 'I'll phone next week when the rates are cheap. I want to hear more about your doctor.'

'More? But I haven't said anything about him,' Julie protested.

'I know,' Meg agreed. 'That's why I want to know about him. You can tell me when I phone.'

'There's nothing to tell,' Julie said untruthfully. 'Bye, Meg—Nick—Ryan. I'm so glad you came; it's been a super weekend.'

She meant it, but as she went up to her bedsitter she found herself thinking that, in spite of everything, she was glad that she had made the move, taken the step. In spite of everything—and that, of course, she admitted honestly, meant Dr Adam Brent.

Next morning, when she reached her office, the night sister had a message for her. 'Dr Brent asked if you would ring him as soon as you came on duty,' she said. Her heart sinking, Julie rang the cottage number.

'Sister Maynard here, Dr Brent,' she said, and she hoped that her voice was cool and professional. 'You wanted me to ring you?'

'Yes, Sister, I want to see you. I'll be right over,' Adam Brent said. Perhaps he wants to make sure I don't tell anyone, Julie thought. As if I would!

Five minutes later Adam Brent strode in. Julie, setting out the medication for the day, finished counting out Miss Clifford's anti-inflammatories and then looked up.

'Sorry, Dr Brent,' she said, annoyed to find that her voice was less than steady.

'Quite all right, Sister,' he said, adding, 'I tried to phone you yesterday, but you were out.'

'Yes, I was,' Julie returned. 'I was off duty for the weekend, Dr Brent.' One hand brushed that aside.

'I know that,' he said. 'I just wanted to let you know that Dr Hutton at the Clinic wants to do Captain O'Connor's leg this morning. As I said to the captain last week, the graft had to wait until the area was free of infection. It's not going to be an easy job, so he'll have to do it under general anaesthetic. I will, of course, be doing the anaesthetic.'

His eyes met hers. 'I'm sure you know, Sister,' he said levelly, 'that there are greater risks in giving an anaesthetic to an elderly patient.'

Julie knew that very well. If there was a sudden and prolonged drop in blood pressure it could lead to circulatory insufficiency, and the danger of thrombosis or

embolism. And with the captain there was the very real
risk of another stroke. But it was a risk that had to
be taken.

'Yes, I do know,' she said quietly. 'So nothing by
mouth for Captain O'Connor.' She was still wondering
why Adam Brent hadn't just left instructions about this.

'I came up yesterday to tell the captain,' the doctor
said, 'and he's turning difficult about it. Says he won't
have it done unless you are there with him.'

'Oh,' Julie said flatly, uncertain what response he
expected of her. 'But surely he can see that isn't really
possible?'

To her surprise, Adam Brent smiled. 'Oh, it's possible,' he said. 'I've talked to Matron. Sister Morkel can
look after your floor, as well as her own, for the morning.
That's what I wanted to let you know yesterday.'

'But Dr Hutton won't want someone else in his
theatre,' Julie said. 'Someone who isn't part of
the team.'

'It's all right with him,' Adam Brent assured her.
'Remember, I'm part of the team and I've told him that
his patient will be easier to handle if you're there with
him. I know—I could just have told the captain it
couldn't be done, and he'd probably have accepted that
but, well, I'm sure you know we do have a different
approach from a big hospital. This is his home as well.'
He looked at his watch.

'I'll be back in half an hour,' he said briskly. 'You
and the captain will go in the ambulance. I'll take my
car so that you and I can come back when the op is over.'

At the door he turned as if to say something else, but
he seemed to change his mind.

Just time to hand out the morning medication, Julie
thought, relieved that Adam Brent had said nothing personal. Relieved, and yet she couldn't help feeling as if

there was still that sword of Damocles, hanging over her head.

'So we're off for a jaunt, Sister,' Captain O'Connor said cheerfully when she went into his room to make sure that he was ready.

'So I believe,' Julie replied.

She helped the old man into his dressing-gown, and then got him into his wheelchair. And now she could see the anxiety under the old man's bright front.

'It's going to be fine, Captain O'Connor,' she said softly. 'I'll be right there with you—as close as they'll let me be—and I'll stay until you come round.'

Cautiously she asked if Dr Brent had said anything about how soon the captain could be brought back to Halvey House.

'Sure and he won't commit himself on that,' the old man said, and his white eyebrows drew together. 'But I can't be blaming him; he'll not be anything but straight with me. He says if everything is fine I can be back later today, but if there's any problem they'll be keeping me there. I reckon that's fair enough.'

The short journey through the early morning city in the ambulance took them to the Clinic before eight, and as the ambulance driver helped Julie to push the wheelchair down the ramp Adam Brent was there beside them.

'I came down yesterday and saw to all the formalities,' he said. 'We can go straight in.'

The reception area was more like a hotel than a hospital, Julie found herself thinking, but the ward had a reassuringly familiar feel. She was given a green theatre gown and a mask, and when she had changed into that she went back to where Captain O'Connor was already on a trolley, beginning to be drowsy from his pre-med.

She sat beside him, answering when he talked to her

and sitting quietly when he closed his eyes, until it was time to take him to the theatre.

It was more than two years since she had done any theatre work, but the busy, charged atmosphere took her right back. The theatre nurses moved the old man onto the operating table and Adam Brent, gowned and masked, nodded to Julie.

'I want to see Sister Sunshine,' Captain O'Connor said with difficulty and, beneath the mask, Julie felt her cheeks grow warm.

The specialist—an older man—indicated where Julie was to stand, and she took her place.

The old man looked across at Julie. Knowing that it was completely unprofessional and knowing, too, that it was only her eyes he could see above the theatre mask, she winked. He managed a slight nod, and then his eyes closed.

The theatre team worked swiftly and efficiently, turning the old man over as soon as he was unconscious so that skin could be taken from the donor area—the buttock. Julie had moved back, now that Captain O'Connor was unconscious, but she could see the fine gauze dressing being applied and then the pressure bandage—after the incisions had been made and the skin removed. Then the work of attaching the small flap of skin to the wound area began. She had never seen a skin graft done, and she was fascinated as the surgeon worked neatly and precisely.

And all the time Adam Brent stood at the top of the table, monitoring the old man's condition—checking that the blood pressure remained normal and that there was no excessive or over-rapid infusion, which could, Julie knew, cause pulmonary swelling.

'That's it,' Dr Hutton said at last, checking the dressing. He looked at Adam. 'Have to see, now, how it takes. These shin jobs are tricky, and his circulation is particularly poor.'

Julie went with the theatre nurse to the recovery room, and sat down beside the trolley the old man was on. She hadn't been there long when Adam Brent, still in his green theatre gown, came in.

'No question of him getting back until Ken Hutton takes off the dressing in twenty-four hours,' he said, his voice low. 'The leg must be immobilised until then, and Ken says he won't risk having him moved.' He looked at the big clock on the wall. 'I'm doing another anaesthetic right now. By the time I finish he should be conscious enough to know you're there. I'll come back and tell him he has to stay here, then we'll leave.'

Once or twice, in the next hour, the captain stirred restlessly, and Julie moved closer so that he could see her. But it was only when Adam Brent came back in that the old man opened his eyes.

'Sister Sunshine,' he murmured. 'So I'm still in the land of the living, am I?'

'You certainly are, you old rogue,' Adam Brent said, with an open affection which took Julie by surprise. 'Now listen, Captain. I'm going to take your Sister Sunshine back to Halvey House now. I'm afraid you're going to have to stay here for a couple of days.'

The old man murmured something and Julie leaned closer, just in time to hear him before he closed his eyes again.

'What did he say?' Adam Brent asked.

Julie couldn't help smiling. 'He said there's not much he can do about that right now,' she told him. The doctor looked down at the old man.

'He's a game old fellow,' he murmured, almost to himself. 'I've grown very fond of him.'

I can see that, Julie thought, but she didn't say anything.

'We'd better get back,' Adam said. 'They'll keep him in the recovery room for another couple of hours, then take him to the ward.' Then, a little awkwardly, he said, 'They'll look after him well, Sister.'

On the way back she asked him more about the procedure of the skin graft, and he told her that, because of the site, it was a free graft.

'A pedicle graft is attached to the donor site?' Julie asked, and he nodded.

'The advantage of this thin split-thickness—which this type of graft is called—is that the donor site heals readily, and that's important for an old person particularly. The disadvantages are that the contracture is great, there is little resistance to trauma and it's cosmetically poor.'

'I shouldn't think that would worry Captain O'Connor,' Julie commented.

When he smiles, she thought, he looks quite different. Younger—so much more approachable.

'I'm sure you're right,' he agreed. He drew up outside the big house.

'Thank you, Dr Brent,' Julie said formally. 'I'll get back to my patients now.' She got out of the car.

'Sister Maynard,' Adam Brent said. Julie turned. This is it, she thought. Now he's going to say something. He was leaning out of the open car window.

'I'll be along to see your folks this afternoon,' he said. 'You'd probably better let Miss Clifford and Mrs Smit know how the captain is.'

'I'll do that,' Julie replied. He nodded and then drove off round to the back, where he kept his station-wagon parked.

He isn't going to say anything, Julie realised. He's going to behave as if nothing happened; as if he didn't kiss me, and I didn't respond the way I did. She lifted her chin.

All right, Adam Brent, she thought. If that's the way you want it we'll do just that, and that's fine by me. But, for one treacherous moment, she found herself wondering if Adam Brent could really forget that kiss. Because she knew very well that she would not be able to.

CHAPTER FOUR

IT TOOK Julie some time to convince little Miss Clifford that the captain was all right, and that he would be coming back to Halvey House in a day or so.

'I didn't say goodbye properly to him, you see, Sister,' she said tremulously. 'I was having breakfast when he went, and it takes me so long to be able to move much first thing in the morning. By the time Nurse Solomon helped me out of bed you and the doctor and the captain had gone.'

Julie explained that they had had to get Captain O'Connor to the Clinic in good time for his operation, and added she was sure he would understand that at that time in the morning other patients wouldn't be around to say goodbye to him.

'And Mrs Smit?' Miss Clifford asked suspiciously. 'I'm sure she would have managed to see him, now that she's moving around on crutches so easily.'

'No, Mrs Smit wasn't there to say goodbye to the captain either,' Julie assured her, and Miss Clifford gave a satisfied little nod.

'Anyway, she'll be going home fairly soon, I suppose. You'll let me know in good time when he's coming back, now, Sister,' she told Julie. 'I would like to do something special—put some flowers or a Welcome card or something in his room.'

She sniffed. 'Not that I'll be the only one doing that, of course,' she said.

Mrs Smit, it turned out, wasn't worried about not seeing the captain to say goodbye. 'I had a nice little visit with him yesterday afternoon,' she told Julie, 'after the doctor came to tell him the operation would be today.' She smiled innocently. 'I must remember to tell Miss Clifford that. I think she must have been asleep; such a pity she missed joining us.'

Julie thought it better to turn a deaf ear to that.

'You're coming on nicely with the crutches, Mrs Smit,' she said. 'I would say you've made faster progress than Mrs Ngalo, although, of course, her hip replacement was done a week after yours.'

'I've always been strong and active, Sister,' Mrs Smit said. 'You have to be when you're a farmer's wife in the Karoo.' For a moment her face was shadowed.

'I wanted to go home sooner,' she said, her voice low. 'I could manage on crutches, I'm sure I could, but my son and my daughter-in-law say they would be too worried. We're over a hundred kilometres from the nearest town, and Piet says they would be worried in case anything went wrong. And, of course, Rietta—my daughter-in-law—has a lot to do. She won't want to take on looking after me as well. Now they're talking about me staying on for a bit in town with my cousin and his wife.'

'There's no reason for anything to go wrong at this stage, Mrs Smit,' Julie told her. 'The soft tissue has had plenty chance to heal. All right, it will take some time to build up muscle tone and, until then, you must be careful not to overexert yourself. Frequent short walks could do nothing but good. Maybe Dr Brent could have a word with your son.'

Mrs Smit shook her head. 'Piet is like his father—as stubborn as they come. Once he makes his mind up that's it. My Pieter—Big Piet—would have said just the same. "You stay there until you're properly better, Johanna." But I miss the farm, Sister, and I miss the children.' She smiled, and the shadows were gone. 'And, since I haven't any choice about being here, I do miss the captain—he makes everything a lot brighter! I'll be glad when he comes back.'

All the same, I'll talk to Adam Brent, Julie decided back in her office.

'I'll certainly have a word with Piet Smit next time he comes,' the doctor said that afternoon, 'but I think his mother has his measure. He's made up his mind that she should be properly better before they take her home. They can certainly afford it—last year was a good one for farmers. And it isn't as if she's unhappy here, with her little flirtation with the captain and her rivalry for his affections with Miss Clifford.'

Julie hesitated. 'I was just wondering,' she said, slowly, 'if there is some problem between Mrs Smit and her daughter-in-law. She hasn't said anything, but somehow I just get that feeling—'

It seemed a little foolish, put into words, but the concern in Adam Brent's grey eyes helped her to go on.

'She's an independent lady, Mrs Smit, and she's pretty strong-willed. I've only met her daughter-in-law once, but she strikes me as something of the same. So there could be a clash, and Mrs Smit may be too proud to say how much she wants to go home,' Julie said. The doctor nodded.

'You could be right,' he said. 'She's not ready yet, I'm afraid. I'd like her to have at least another week of daily physiotherapy—once she's back on the farm she won't be able to have that—but there's no reason why she shouldn't be able to go home in ten days at the outside. Perhaps you could talk some more to Mrs Smit—see if you can find out if you're right and if there is a problem.'

He smiled, and Julie thought again how much more approachable he looked when he smiled. Which he did fairly often at just about everyone but her, she had to admit.

'If anyone can get Mrs Smit to let it all hang out, it's you,' he said surprisingly. She felt her cheeks grow warm.

'I'll certainly try,' she murmured.

Adam Brent had been sitting on the edge of her desk. He stood up now. 'Better do my rounds,' he said. 'Have you time to come in with me to Miss Clifford?'

As always, Miss Clifford's face lit up when they went into her room.

Gently the doctor took the red, swollen hands in his. And, gentle as he was, the old lady winced.

'Still painful and stiff, in spite of the change in the anti-inflammatories, Miss Clifford,' he commented.

'I think a little better, Dr Brent,' Miss Clifford said. 'And the cold packs that Sister and Nurse Solomon put on do help. More than the exercises the physiotherapist makes me do, I'm sure.'

Adam patted her hand. 'You know she's keeping your exercises as gentle as possible, Miss Clifford,' he told her, 'but we do want to preserve the joint function.'

For a moment his eyes met Julie's, and the unsaid words were there.

For as long as possible.

'On the other hand, I think it's reasonable to have you miss her visit on a really bad day.' He stood up.

'Can I rely on you to be honest with Sister Maynard? If it's possible I do want you to have your session of physiotherapy. But if you really don't feel up to it you tell Sister. Is that a deal?'

'It's a deal, Dr Brent,' the old lady agreed. 'Sister, would you change that tape for me before you go?'

Julie took the tape out of the cassette machine.

'What would you like now, Miss Clifford?' she asked, putting *Swan Lake* back in its box.

'*Les Sylphides*, I think,' Miss Clifford said. Julie put it on, delighted, as always, by the immediate pleasure on the old lady's face as the music began.

'One of my favourite roles,' Miss Clifford murmured. She looked at the doctor. 'Tell me, Dr Brent, has that little girl of yours started ballet lessons yet?' Adam shook his head.

'She's only seven,' he said. 'Maybe next year—'

'She should have started a year or two ago,' Miss Clifford told him firmly. 'Tell me, when did you start ballet lessons, Sister?'

Julie felt her cheeks grow warm, remembering that time when Adam had come in and found her doing a pirouette for Miss Clifford.

'When I was six,' she replied. And then, with honesty, she added, 'But I didn't make much of it, Miss Clifford.'

The snowy white head nodded, ignoring her second comment.

'You get her started, Dr Brent, and she can come up here to show me how she's doing. I'll keep her right. I could do that, you know, even without being able to show her.'

'I'm sure you could, Miss Clifford,' the doctor agreed. 'I'll think about it.'

At the door he turned back. 'I wish I had seen you dance,' he said softly, and the old lady's cheeks flushed with pleasure.

Adam glanced down at Julie, as they walked back along the corridor.

'I know,' he said, and he smiled. 'It's only dreams, but people need dreams sometimes.' And then, almost as if he'd regretted saying that, he went on 'Anything else you want to discuss, Sister?'

'Mrs Johnson in Ward Seven, Dr Brent,' Julie said as they went into her office. 'I know her medication had to be increased because of the pain she had after the lower limb amputation, but she seems to be more confused, more agitated, than she was before. And she has lost weight.'

Dr Brent nodded.

'I was half expecting that,' he said. 'We'll have to change the dosage. I don't mean to sound like a lecturer but in any drug regimen for elderly people you have to bear in mind that drugs can alter the nutritional status, which might already be affected. And we'll have to juggle the pain control because there's no need for her to be confused. Do you have her chart there?'

Julie handed it to him, and he wrote on it.

'Half a tablet—instead of one—morning and midday, and we'll see how that goes. Leave the night dosage a full tablet. And let me know what you think—you're in a better position than I am to assess her.'

I know that, Julie thought when he had gone. But it felt good, very good, that Adam Brent had said it. And meant it, she knew.

Matron confirmed that when she came up to Julie's floor next day.

'Dr Brent was telling me that he has great faith in your judgement of the patients, Sister Maynard,' she said, putting down the chart she had been looking at. She smiled. 'I'm sure you must have been aware that he had some doubts about your appointment at first.'

Julie knew that her cheeks were warm. 'I—yes, I was aware of that, Matron,' she replied a little awkwardly. And that is the understatement of the year, she thought. 'I think he felt my lack of geriatric experience was a drawback,' she said carefully. Matron nodded.

'That, and the fact that you're an attractive young woman,' she said, taking Julie by surprise. 'I think it's safe to say that Dr Brent is more comfortable with older people.'

Afterwards Julie wondered if she should have said as much as she did. But there was sympathy in

Matron's blue eyes, and concern in her voice.

'What I really mind,' she said with some difficulty, 'is that Dr Brent made up his mind about me without giving me a chance to prove myself.' It was a moment or two before the older woman replied.

'Yes, I know that.'

So, Adam Brent had obviously talked to Matron and told her how he felt about this new Sister.

'It was a very difficult time for Dr Brent when his wife died,' Matron said unexpectedly. 'It's almost two years ago now, but—'

It was a strange thing to say, Julie thought. Of course it must have been difficult for Adam Brent, losing his wife—it would be for any man. But there was something about the way Matron said it. . . She stood up.

'I'd better get back to my office,' she said briskly.

She glanced out the window. 'A black south-easter,' she said. 'Looks as if we might be in for a storm.'

The top of Table Mountain was covered in heavy black clouds, and any time Julie looked out through the afternoon she saw that the clouds were rolling further down the mountain until, by the time she went off duty, it had almost disappeared.

'I thought I'd come to a winter rainfall area,' she said to the night sister when she was handing over. 'It's only the end of February—I didn't expect anything like this until winter.'

'Oh, we can get summer storms as well,' Night Sister assured her. 'Not often, but certainly often enough to justify the name of Cape of Storms for a good part of the year!'

There was something exhilarating about the coolness after all the summer heat, and about the sudden fierce gusts blowing the trees and the big striped umbrellas out on the lawn. From her office window Julie could see the gardener struggling to take the big umbrellas down and put them on the stoep.

As soon as she had finished handing over she hurried up to her small flat and changed into jeans, a T-shirt and sandals. Then, not waiting for the lift, she ran down the three flights of stairs and out into the garden.

She could hear thunder rumbling around the mountain and then suddenly—spectacularly—the darkened sky was lit up by bright sheet lightning, followed by another deep rumble of thunder, as she followed the path that led round to the swimming pool. The first drops of rain began to fall, driving her under one of the big old oak trees. Only to find Adam Brent there, taking shelter too. He recovered before she did.

'Another orphan of the storm, Sister,' he said when she stopped in her tracks. 'Come on in, it's a little drier here.'

Another bright flash of lightning illuminated the tree, the garden and the big old house.

'You're pretty wet already,' Adam said, and Julie was all too conscious of her wet T-shirt clinging to her.

When the next rumble of thunder was over and the rain came down harder than ever, he looked down at her.

'I'm going to make a run for home,' he said. 'Beauty is with the children, but Catherine doesn't like storms. You'd better come with me—you can dry off there. This rain won't last much longer.'

The cottage was only marginally nearer than the run across the lawn back to the big house, Julie knew. But it was a gesture of—conciliation, perhaps.

'Come on—run,' Adam Brent said, taking her assent for granted. He took her hand and they ran together up the path, slippery now with the sudden rain. They were both breathless when they reached the cottage.

The moment Adam opened the door Catherine's small figure hurled itself at him. He lifted her up and held her close to him, not saying anything, and she buried

her face against him. After a while she lifted her head
and looked at Julie, seemingly unsurprised by her
being there.

'I wasn't really frightened,' she said. 'It's just the
loud noise of the thunder I don't like.'

'I like the thunder,' the little boy, David, said, but
Julie noticed that he had one chubby little hand firmly
in the big dog's collar. 'I'm just helping Shandy not to
be nervous.'

'I'm not surprised at anyone being nervous,' Julie
said. 'That last clap of thunder was quite something.'

Adam Brent, still with Catherine in his arms,
looked at her.

'You're soaked,' he said, rather unnecessarily, Julie
felt. 'David, get that towelling robe of mine, and take
Sister Maynard to the bathroom so that she can change.'

He set Catherine down. 'Catherine, could you ask
Beauty to put the kettle on? Then she can go.'

The blue towelling robe was quite a bit too big for
Julie. She stripped to her pants and bra and put it on,
tying the belt firmly and rolling up the sleeves. She
rubbed her hair as dry as possible, and then went back
to the big living-room.

Adam had changed into tracksuit trousers and a
T-shirt. His hair was rumpled, and, like her own, not
entirely dry. He was just setting down a tray with a big
brown teapot on it and some mugs.

'I could have gone back to my flat,' Julie said, feeling
very self-conscious.

'I know,' he agreed, 'but this was nearer, and, well,
I promised Catherine and David we'd ask you to come
for tea. They seem to want to show you all sorts of
things.'

Catherine's eyes, grey like her father's and long-
lashed, were on Julie.

'I didn't know your hair was so pretty,' she said shyly.

'It was tied back the other day. It makes you look like a princess now. Daddy, did you know Julie's hair was long and curly like that?'

For a moment, before Adam turned away to set out the mugs on the tray, Julie was all too conscious of that night when he had seen her with her hair loose on her bare shoulders—that night when he had kissed her.

'Yes,' he said, but quietly and not in the old brusque way she had expected. 'Yes, I did know.'

Carefully, but easily—as if, Julie thought with a strange and disturbing pang, he had done this so many times—he poured tea, milky for his children and each mug with a spoonful of sugar in it.

'Sugar for you, Sister Maynard?'

'No thank you, just milk,' Julie said, and at the same time little David laughed.

'Daddy, you can't say "Sister Maynard", not when Catherine and me say Julie. It sounds like you don't know each other.'

Adam Brent smiled, and there was the same shyness—surprising in him, and oddly touching—that there had been in his small daughter's smile.

'All right, then, if Sister Maynard doesn't mind—Julie.'

'And you have to call Daddy Adam, cos that's his name,' David told Julie. 'It's acksherly Adam Richard, but Adam will do. Go on, say it.'

Adam handed Julie a mug of tea.

'Thank you—Adam,' Julie said, with a feeling of unreality that she should be sitting here in Adam Brent's house, wearing his dressing-gown, taking a mug of tea from him—and calling him Adam. It made her feel rather as if she were taking part in some Mad Hatter's Teaparty.

'I've finished my tea,' Catherine said very soon. She

held out her hand to Julie. 'Please come and see where my Blue Ted sleeps.'

Julie finished her own tea, and went with the little girl along the passage and into a pretty, rose-sprigged room at the far end. There was a small wooden cot set beside the bed, and in it lay the blue teddy Julie had mended.

'I see he's still wearing his red ribbon,' Julie said. 'He's lucky to have such a nice bed.'

'It isn't really his,' Catherine told her. 'It belongs to Angela Mary Felicity. My granny gave me Angela Mary Felicity, and Grandad made the bed. But it's all right for Blue Ted to have the bed sometimes.'

Angela Mary Felicity, with flaxen curls, big blue eyes and dimples, was sitting at a small desk. Her dress looked like a miniature Laura Ashley style.

'She's beautiful,' Julie said.

'Yes, but she isn't cuddly like Blue Ted,' Catherine said. And then quickly, and with an anxious glance at the doll, she said, 'I do love her, Julie, but I love Blue Ted for different things. Mummy gave him to me when I was just a baby, you see.' For a moment there was a shadow on the little girl's face, then it was gone.

'I'm sure Angela Mary Felicity doesn't mind,' Julie assured her, a momentary tightness in her throat. 'What a lovely dolls' house, Catherine.'

They looked at the dolls' house, and Julie was allowed to lift out the tiny occupants.

'You can put them back in any room you want,' Catherine told her, and she leaned her chin on her small brown hands as she watched Julie setting the mother and the father and the children in the seats beside the piano.

A little later, going back to the big, comfortable living-room, Julie stopped at the door. Adam Brent was down on the floor, helping his small son to build a Lego castle.

'We need a turret here, David,' he said, absorbed, 'so that they can watch out for enemies coming. You put the blue blocks on next.'

He watched as David built up the tower, the small fingers struggling to fit the blocks together. Gently his own big brown hand covered the child's, and he showed him how to do it. Julie, watching, felt once again that strange and disturbing pang.

Adam looked up. 'Sorry,' he said, his confusion lending a vulnerability to the man Julie had been so sure she knew. He got to his feet.

'Would you like more tea?' he asked. 'I'm afraid Catherine rushed you into finishing.' Julie shook her head.

'No, thank you,' she said. She looked out the window. The rain had stopped. 'I'd better get back while it's fair.'

'Your clothes are dry—I put them in the tumble-drier,' Adam said. He went through to the kitchen, and came back with her jeans and her T-shirt. Julie changed in the bathroom and came back through, saying goodbye to the children and to the big golden dog—who sat down and solemnly gave her a paw.

'The storm seems to be over,' she said at the door. 'It took me by surprise—although it shouldn't have, since the old sailors did call this the Cape of Storms.'

Adam Brent looked down at her. 'You'll see plenty storms in winter,' he said. 'If you're still here, that is.' Julie lifted her chin.

'Yes, I'll be here,' she said clearly.

And as she walked back to the big house she couldn't help thinking that the words had sounded like a promise.

But a promise to herself, or to Adam Brent?

CHAPTER FIVE

'FLOWERS,' Mrs Smit said decisively. 'That's what we need. The captain loves flowers.'

'And a "Welcome Home" banner,' Miss Clifford insisted. 'He would like that, I know he would. And I've known him longer than you have, Mrs Smit.'

She sat up as straight as she could in her wheelchair and glared up at Mrs Smit, whose position on crutches was more commanding. It was time to intervene, Julie thought.

'I'm sure Captain O'Connor would love to have flowers and a banner waiting in his room,' she suggested. She could see that neither Mrs Smit nor Miss Clifford was prepared to give an inch.

'And I'm even more sure,' she said clearly, 'that neither of you would want to spoil his return for him in any way.' Miss Clifford coloured, and Mrs Smit looked away.

'No, of course not, Sister,' Miss Clifford said a little faintly.

'Mrs Smit, you're so good with flowers—would you manage to go out in the garden with Peter and get him to cut what you want?' Julie suggested. Mrs Smit nodded.

'And you're so artistic, Miss Clifford,' she said graciously. 'Is there time for you to make a banner?' Miss Clifford looked a little embarrassed.

'Actually,' she admitted, 'I've almost finished making it. I got Nurse Solomon to get some nice stiff paper yesterday.'

Julie held her breath, but Mrs Smit was prepared to let that go.

'When do we expect the captain, Sister?' she asked.

'In about an hour,' Julie told her. 'Dr Brent is bringing him back when he finishes at the Clinic, and he said they didn't have a long list in the theatre today.'

She went down in the lift with Mrs Smit and left her with Peter, the gardener. When she got back to the ward Miss Clifford, with Prudence Solomon's help, had got the banner spread out. Where had she managed to hide it? Julie wondered, amused. With felt-tip pens carefully held in her swollen hands, she was putting the finishing touches to WELCOME HOME, CAPTAIN.

'I don't think it matters that I've just said "Captain", Sister,' she said anxiously. 'I couldn't manage to write any more.'

'I think it looks fine, Miss Clifford,' Julie reassured her.

And, a little later, she said the same to Mrs Smit when the big bowl of flowers was arranged on the table at the window.

'And just in time, here's Dr Brent's car now,' she told both her patients.

She watched as Adam Brent took the folding wheel-chair from the back of his estate car, helped the old captain into it and pushed the chair up the ramp and into the house. A few moments later the lift door opened.

'Captain O'Connor, it's lovely to have you back,' Julie said, going to meet them.

'And grand it is to be back, Sister Sunshine,' the old man returned. Quite deliberately he winked as he said that, but Adam Brent only smiled.

'Let's get you to your room, Captain,' he said. 'It's been quite a day already for you.' He turned to Julie and smiled. 'Only a week he was there, but you should have seen the round-up of nurses and patients waiting to say goodbye to him!'

'You made yourself popular, did you, Captain?' Julie asked.

'You could say that,' the captain agreed.

They had reached the door of his room, and Adam stopped.

'Well, now,' the old man said softly, as he looked at the big bowl of flowers and the banner behind it. 'Well, now, I wasn't expecting anything like this.'

'Welcome home, Captain,' Miss Clifford and Mrs Smit said together. Captain O'Connor coughed, and took a handkerchief from his dressing-gown pocket.

'Must have caught a cold at that place,' he said accusingly, and he blew his nose.

For a moment Adam's grey eyes met Julie's, and Julie could see that he was as touched as she was—not only by the welcome, but by the old man's reaction to it.

Mrs Smit recovered first. 'And how are you feeling, Captain?' she asked him. 'Is your leg recovering?'

'My leg isn't too bad at all,' the old man replied. 'They seem to feel that this patching business has a good chance of working. But as for my b—' He stopped. 'As for the place they took the patch from,' he said solemnly, but there was mischief in his eyes, 'I'm finding that sitting is not too comfortable.' He looked up at Julie. 'No doubt the folks at the Clinic will be telling you, Sister, that I'm to lie on me front for a bit when the—other area is complaining.'

'I would expect that, Captain,' Julie assured him. She looked at Adam. 'I thought, Dr Brent, that Miss Clifford and Mrs Smit could, perhaps, have a cup of tea with Captain O'Connor, and then it might be a good idea to get him into bed for a rest.'

'Sounds fine, Sister,' Adam Brent agreed. He looked at his watch. 'If you were thinking of that right away, I've just time to join you.'

It was a proper little party, Julie thought later, for she

had asked Matron if they could have a small cake instead of the usual biscuits that came in the afternoon. Miss Clifford's cheeks were as pink as the icing on the cake, and she and Mrs Smit were positively warm to each other as they listened to the old man's stories of his stay in the Clinic.

'And, would you believe it, ladies,' he said solemnly, 'every day they come around with a menu, and you choose what you want for lunch and dinner. That's once you're over your operation or whatever, of course. But it's a fine place, is it not, Dr Brent?'

'Yes, it is,' Adam Brent agreed.

'And a glass of wine, if you want it, when you're getting better,' the captain went on. 'Is it not a pity we don't do that here at Halvey House now, Sister?'

'Perhaps it is,' Julie said. 'But the Clinic is a private one, remember, and people are usually there for only a short time.'

She stood up, and so did Adam Brent, looking at his watch as he did so.

'I'll be in later to see you,' he said to the old man.

Julie walked along the corridor with him to the lift.

'Ken Hutton is cautious, but he thinks it's looking good,' he said. 'The donor site is healing nicely—in spite of what the old rogue was saying to try to shock his lady friends—and the graft itself seems to have taken well. One of the dangers of this sort of graft in such a position—on the shin—is that there is little resistance to trauma but, with him being in his wheelchair, there's less danger of that. It's just something we have to be conscious of.'

He gave Julie further instructions about the dressing as they stood at the open door of the lift.

'Unlike the captain, you didn't catch cold,' he said, and smiled. 'With getting wet the other day, I mean.'

Unbidden came the memory of standing at the door

in his house, wearing his towelling dressing-gown and watching him pouring tea for his children—his big hands careful on the china teapot. A memory which Julie found strangely disturbing.

'No,' she said, colouring. 'No, I—I didn't catch cold.'

When he had gone she walked back along the corridor, and found herself thinking how different it was to be working with Adam Brent without the barrier of his disapproval between them.

Much as Captain O'Connor was enjoying his welcome-home party, she could see—when Miss Clifford and Mrs Smit had gone and he was in bed—that he was tired.

'Yes, I am that, Sister,' he admitted when she said that. 'Not that there's any reason to be, and me living in the lap of luxury in the Clinic.'

'It's the anaesthetic,' Julie explained as she adjusted a pillow to make him more comfortable. 'And you were under for quite a while, remember. Your whole system has a reaction to that. It can take some time to recover from it.'

'And me not just in the first flush of youth, either,' the old man agreed cheerfully. 'Ah, well, I won't be complaining about the tiredness, then, Sister. And I'm not complaining, either, because they kept me in for a week. Dr Brent and Dr Hutton explained well enough that it was necessary.'

A little later, when Julie looked in, he was fast asleep. And so was Miss Clifford, in her room further along. But Mrs Smit was sitting in a chair, reading a magazine.

'It has good recipes in it, this *Sarie*,' she said a little defensively. 'In Afrikaans, of course, but you won't have much Afrikaans, coming from Durban.'

'Enough to follow a recipe, I think,' Julie said, glancing at the magazine. 'Tomato chutney—looks good. Are you planning on making it when you get home?'

The older woman's hands were suddenly still.

'Yes, I suppose I am,' she said, her voice low. With an effort she smiled. 'Elize, my granddaughter, likes to help when I cook. But I'm not sure that her mother likes her helping me. She keeps saying she doesn't want the children to be a nuisance, but I love having them with me.'

Julie hesitated. 'Have you told her that?' she asked gently.

Mrs Smit paused.

'I don't find it easy to talk to Rietta,' she said after a moment. 'She has her own way of doing things, you know. She's very quick, very independent.'

'But just to tell her that you don't find the children a nuisance—that you miss them now?' Julie suggested.

'She isn't easy to talk to,' Mrs Smit said again.

And I don't think you are either, Julie thought, giving up for the moment.

'But I think I'll try to have a word with Rietta, her daughter-in-law,' she said to Adam when he came up to the ward later. 'She's coming in a couple of days.' He thought that was a good idea.

'But you know, of course,' he said, hesitantly, 'that you're taking this way beyond anything that is expected of you in your job. I mean—Mrs Smit will go out of here in a week, whether she goes to the farm or to her brother. Your responsibility doesn't go any beyond that.'

'I know that,' Julie agreed. Now she hesitated, but only for a moment. 'Do you think I'm interfering, Dr Brent? Is that what you mean? Do you think it would be better just to leave the whole thing?'

'No, I don't think that at all,' Adam said, with such certainty that she couldn't doubt him. 'I suppose I'm just—surprised that you should feel that you have to do something to help.'

He hadn't said the words, but Julie was sure that they

were in his mind. A girl like you. A girl he had so
unfairly classified on their first meeting.

She stood silent, shaken by the knot of unhappiness
in her throat and by the sting of tears behind her eyes.
Why should I care what this man thinks of me? she told
herself, and she lifted her chin.

Then slowly he smiled—a smile that lit up his face,
a smile that had something of his small son's mischief
in it and something of his daughter's intensity.

'But I shouldn't be surprised,' he said. 'I should know,
by now, that Sister Sunshine doesn't leave her job when
she leaves her ward. So, good luck to you, Sister, with
Mrs Smit and her daughter-in-law.'

Julie was too taken aback to accompany him when
he nodded, and turned away. But at the door he stopped.

'Another of your good ideas,' he said, and he was
still smiling. 'Matron says you've talked to her about
letting the children and Shandy come to the stoep to
visit any of the patients who are out. I've said I'll bring
them down this afternoon at teatime. Will you be there?'

'If I can,' Julie replied. 'Depends how things are up
here, and if I can leave Prudence in charge.'

The ward was quiet that afternoon and she was able
to leave Prudence, with instructions to bleep her if she
was needed. Mrs Smit was already down on the stoep,
and so was Ted Ramsay and Miss Clifford. Julie took
Captain O'Connor down with her in his wheelchair.
She'd been a little doubtful, but had given in to his
insistence that it was fresh air and a change of scene
that he needed.

'You get plenty fresh air in your open window,
Captain,' she pointed out as they went down in the lift.
He sighed so pathetically that she had to smile.

'Well, then, it's the loneliness that's getting to me,'
he said. And added, looking up at her, 'And I wouldn't
like to be disappointing the ladies, and them having

missed my company while I was in the Clinic.'

'No, it would be a shame to disappoint them, wouldn't it?' Julie agreed as the lift reached the ground floor.

Her own patients, and a few from each of the other floors, were sitting comfortably on the wide shady stoep as one of the nursing aides from the first floor poured tea and handed the cups round.

Julie set the captain's chair beside the couch on which Mrs Smit was sitting, with Miss Clifford's chair on his other side.

'Do have a biscuit, Captain,' Miss Clifford said. 'See, they're your favourite shortbread ones.'

Mrs Smit leaned over and patted the captain's hand. 'I wish I could bring you some of my own home-made *melktert*. I know you would enjoy it.' She looked at Miss Clifford. 'I suppose you wouldn't ever have done much in the baking line, Miss Clifford?'

Miss Clifford coloured.

'Not much, because my life was too busy, Mrs Smit. But—but I did make delicious ginger biscuits. All the other dancers used to love them.'

'Sure and both the *melktert* and the ginger biscuits would be a wonderful thing,' the old man said gallantly. 'Well, now, what's this?'

Julie had already seen Adam coming along the path, with Shandy walking sedately on the lead, and David and Catherine—obviously on their best behaviour— hand in hand beside him.

'We've come to join you for tea,' Adam said. 'Sit, Shandy.'

The big golden Labrador sat down but his tail went on wagging, and his head turned from side to side as Adam took David and Catherine around the patients, introducing them.

David wasn't at all shy, and in a moment he was asking Captain O'Connor eagerly about the ships he

had sailed on and if he had ever been in a shipwreck.
Catherine, Julie could see, found it harder to meet all
these people, most of them strangers. Seeing her awkwardness, Julie went over to her and stayed beside her
as they talked to one of the old ladies from the first
floor. Then, taking Catherine's hand in hers, she took
her over to Miss Clifford.

'Miss Clifford was a ballerina, Catherine,' she told
the little girl. 'She can tell you about lots of famous
ballet dancers.'

'I used to teach little girls, Catherine,' Miss Clifford
said. 'Are you going to have ballet lessons soon? I keep
telling your daddy it's time you started.'

Catherine nodded. 'Next term I'm going to start,' she
said, still shy and her small hand still holding Julie's
tightly.

'Will you come and show me when you start?' the
old lady asked her.

'Yes, I will,' Catherine said. And then, her shyness
forgotten, 'Look, Julie, Shandy's saying hello to
everyone.'

The dog, obviously feeling that it was time he took
part in all this, was going round the group of old people,
sitting down beside each one and solemnly offering a
large paw. When the paw was duly shaken and his head
patted, he moved on to the next one. Julie, trying to be
unobtrusive about it, kept close as he approached
Captain O'Connor, seeing—as Adam also moved
closer—that neither of them were prepared to risk that
large paw coming in contact with the skin graft on the
old man's leg.

But Shandy, almost as if he knew, just sat down and
very gently lifted his paw, waiting for the old man to
lean forward and return the greeting. Julie only realised
then that she had been holding her breath, and as she

let it out for a moment she found Adam's eyes meeting hers in shared relief.

'You were right, Sister, that was a good idea,' he said a little later, coming over to her. He looked at his watch. 'I have to go to the Clinic now. There are a couple of patients I need to see before tomorrow's operating list. Catherine, I think you and David and Shandy should go back home now. I told Beauty you'd be back around this time.'

'Daddy,' Catherine whispered urgently, 'have you asked Julie?'

'Oh—no, I haven't,' Adam said, taken aback. 'We were only talking about it, Catherine, I don't know if Sister Maynard would—'

'Ask her and see,' Catherine said, not whispering now. Adam gave in, and turned to Julie.

'The children and I were wondering,' he said a little awkwardly, 'if you would like to come with us to the beach on Saturday? I know it's your day off—maybe you've already made plans.'

'No, I haven't,' Julie said slowly, uncertain what she should say to this. But Catherine had taken her hand again.

'Please come, Julie. We can show you our favourite places and, if we're very lucky, we might see seals.'

'Once we saw a whale,' David said, joining in. 'An' you could see the castle Daddy and me are going to make. We make such lovely castles, and we make moats, and the sea water comes in to fill the moat, and—'

Julie burst out laughing.

'Castles and moats I can't resist,' she assured the small boy. 'And I'd love to see seals, Catherine.'

She looked at the big doctor. 'That's if you really want me to come,' she said, all at once uncertain.

'I would like it very much,' Adam said and, although his words were formal, there was a warmth in his eyes that told her that he really meant it. A warmth that made her look forward, more and more, to spending the day with him and his children.

She was ready at nine, Adam having assured her that she didn't need to bring anything other than suntan oil.

'We're well equipped for beach expeditions,' he said as he put her beach towel and her big floppy hat into the back of the car beside a rug and a bright beach umbrella.

'We've got a picnic,' David told her, leaning forward from the back seat. 'Coffee for you and Daddy, and cool drink for me and Catherine. And sandwiches. And it's all right for you to sit in the front seat.'

'Thank you,' Julie said, buckling her seat belt. 'Am I taking someone's turn in the front?'

'My turn, acksherly,' the little boy said. 'But it's all right.'

'You shouldn't even say, David,' Catherine told him fiercely. 'It isn't good manners.'

'But I wanted Julie to know,' David replied, surprised. 'That's why I told her.'

'Thank you, David,' Julie said again. 'I do appreciate you giving me your turn.'

They were going up the coast, Adam told her as they drove away from Halvey House.

'We like the quieter beaches, so that we can take Shandy with us,' he said. 'And you get a wonderful view back to Table Bay, and Table Mountain.'

It was, indeed, a wonderful view, Julie thought half an hour later when they were settled on a quiet stretch of white sand, with the umbrella up and the rug spread underneath it. Already there was a heat haze, and Table Mountain shimmered above the still sea.

'Not a breath of wind—it's going to be hot,' Adam

said. 'Come on, kids, suntan lotion before we start on that castle.'

Julie watched as his big brown hands—the same hands she had seen so often, competent and professional, caring for patients—spread suntan lotion on his small son's brown back and then on Catherine's, before going onto their faces.

'We do have our hats on, Daddy,' Catherine reminded him.

'I know,' Adam said, 'but you still need suntan lotion.'

'Julie can't reach her back,' David said as he lifted his bucket and spade up. 'You'll have to do her back for her, Daddy.'

Julie, busy smoothing suntan lotion on her arms, stopped. Adam Brent's eyes met hers.

'I can manage,' Julie said awkwardly.

'No, you can't,' he returned, equally awkwardly.

He took the tube of lotion from her. 'Turn round,' he told her. Silently, Julie turned her back to him. Then she felt his fingers on her back, smoothing the lotion in with slow, strong strokes.

Slow and strong, and very, very disturbing.

The sea shimmering blue in the heat; the sand warm under her feet; the mountain which seemed to rise straight from the sea across the bay. And Adam Brent's hands warm on her back and her shoulders. Suddenly, foolishly, it was a moment frozen in time—a moment that Julie knew, with a strange certainty, that she would not forget.

With an effort, she moved away.

'Thanks,' she said, and hoped that her voice sounded light, casual. 'That should protect me from the sun.'

'Now you have to do Daddy's back for him,' Catherine told her. 'We're very strict about sun protection, you know.' Funny, old-fashioned little girl,

Julie thought with a rush of affection.

'And a good thing too,' she agreed.

Adam's shoulders and back were a deep golden brown. She would feel these strong muscles when she touched him.

'No, I can do Daddy's back,' David said. 'Sit down, Daddy, so that I can reach you.'

'Thanks, David,' Adam said, sitting down on the rug.

Julie put the cap on her bottle and set it down carefully, telling herself that that was a relief. And conscious that there was something else she was feeling as well as relief. Disappointed? No, that was ridiculous. Of course she wasn't.

'Does Shandy help to dig?' she asked the children as they chose a spot for the castle.

Catherine shook her head. 'No, he just watches,' she said. 'It's funny, though, because he digs holes in the garden when he wants to hide something.'

'He doesn't even need that excuse,' Adam said ruefully. 'He just likes digging. Except when we could use his help.' The big golden dog was sitting with his back to them, studiously looking away.

'You know what,' Julie said, 'it probably bothers him to see you doing something he keeps getting into trouble for.'

'It probably does,' Adam agreed, smiling, and the ease and casual warmth of his smile made Julie even more determined to try to forget that strange and disturbing way she had felt a little while ago.

Adam and his children were obviously a team well experienced in working together to build sandcastles. Under instruction from Catherine and David, Julie obediently dug where she was told to and fetched buckets full of water when the moat was made. But the finer points of construction were left to the experts, and she watched in admiration as turrets and towers rose with intricate flights of steps leading up to them.

'But the water just sinks into the sand,' Catherine said sadly.

'It will fill up when the tide comes in,' Adam told her.

He was finishing a wide flight of steps while David carefully made a path of shells. The little boy's copper-coloured head and his father's brown one were both bent forward, equally absorbed. Julie watched them, and once again she found herself very conscious of the closeness of the bond between Adam and his children. A bond made closer, she thought, by the loss of the woman who should have been with them. Adam's wife. David's and Catherine's mother. So sad, for him and for the children, to lose her.

Adam straightened up and Julie looked away quickly out to sea, very glad of her dark glasses in that moment when he must have seen that she was watching him.

'Is that a seal out there?' she said. Adam stood up.

'No, it's someone in a wetsuit,' he told her. 'Let's walk along to the rocks, and by the time we get back the tide should have reached our moat.'

The children put their buckets and spades under the umbrella. Shandy, at the prospect of a walk, ran ahead eagerly and David ran after him.

'I like your bikini, Julie,' Catherine said seriously. 'I'd like to have a nice flowery bikini just like that when I'm a lady. Bikinis don't look so nice on little girls, you see.'

It wasn't easy, but Julie hoped she had managed to keep her face straight and her voice as serious as Catherine's. 'Well, different, anyway,' she agreed, suddenly all too conscious of the scantiness of that bikini as she picked up her short towelling robe and put it on.

They walked along to an outcrop of rocks, where the dog and the children peered into small pools of water, fascinated. Adam and Julie sat with their backs against

a huge, smooth rock, watching them. Julie closed her
eyes, feeling no pressure to talk—a little surprised at
how much at ease she could feel with Adam Brent after
all that had happened between them.

After a while Adam asked her about her family, and
she told him about her parents, her brothers, the old
dog—Glen—and the young one, Holly.

'We got her as a sort of colleague and successor three
years ago because Glen had kidney problems,' she said.
'But he's taken on a new lease of life now. He eats his
special diet because he knows that if he doesn't Holly
will, and he actually plays with Holly—in an indulgent,
kindly-uncle sort of way.'

The children and the big golden dog were some distance away now, peering into rock pools.

'You were right. I bet Shandy would love her too,'
Adam said, smiling.

He turned to her, and now the smile was gone. 'I
should have said this before, Julie,' he said, with difficulty. 'I'm—not very good at saying I'm sorry, but I'm
saying it now.'

I mustn't misunderstand him, Julie thought. Does he
mean because he judged me without giving me a chance,
or does he mean that night?

'I'm not quite sure what you mean, Adam,' she said
carefully.

He smiled, but the smile didn't reach his eyes.

'I said things to you that were unjustified and unforgivable that night when you came back with your
friends, and you didn't know I was there on the stoep.
I've left it far too long—but I'm saying it now. I'm
sorry, Julie.'

Julie wasn't sure what she murmured, but Adam
seemed to realise that his apology had been accepted.

'That young man—is he someone special?' Adam
asked. Julie shook her head.

'Ryan? No, he's one of a group of friends. He's an intern—we all trained together. We've been friends for years.'

The sound of the waves breaking against the rocks and the distant sounds of laughter from the children made her conscious, now, of the silence between them.

'And is there anyone else who is—special?'

He sounded very casual, and of course he was. It was just the sort of friendly enquiry anyone might make. Julie shook her head, glad that her hair was loose and the long fair curls shielded her face.

'That surprises me,' Adam Brent said. She looked at him.

'You mean—a girl like me?' she asked, unable to stop herself from saying that, but ashamed of herself as she saw the colour leave his face.

'I suppose I deserved that,' he said, his voice low.

Julie clasped her hands round her knees.

'I'm twenty-six, Adam,' she said lightly. 'As well as being old enough to be a sister, I'm old enough to have been around. Yes, there was a doctor, but he met someone else. And there was a patient—well, we didn't start seeing each other until he'd been discharged, of course—but he didn't bother telling me that he was engaged because his fiancée was safely away on a skiing holiday when he came to have his appendix out.'

Mark Elliott. She had been so hurt at the time, so devastated. More hurt than when Tim Curran had told her he had met someone else. Now Mark seemed, in the words of the old song, 'long ago and far away'.

It was, she thought, getting a little heavy somehow, and she was glad when the children came running up to them, breathless, to say that the tide was coming in and surely the moat would be filled up by now.

'We'd better go back, then,' Adam said, smiling.

'I'll be there first,' David said.

'No, you won't,' Catherine returned. 'I can run faster than you.'

'Can't,' her small brother told her. 'Boys can run faster than girls.'

'And dogs can run faster than either,' Adam said ruefully as the children and the dog ran back the way they had come towards the bright umbrella and the castle beside it.

He stood up, and drew Julie to her feet. And then, without releasing her hands, he said, quietly, 'I should apologise, too, for kissing you. But I don't think I can do that. It—wouldn't be honest to say that I'm sorry for that kiss.'

Julie felt the slow, warm colour flooding her cheeks. He must know, she thought, remembering so well, that I can't be sorry for that kiss either.

Even just remembering how her whole body, how everything in her, had responded to being in his arms made her cheeks feel even warmer. She managed to draw her hands back from his.

'You don't need to say sorry for a kiss, Adam,' she said very lightly. Too lightly, perhaps, but the memory still had so much power to leave her shaken that lightness was a defence. 'Come on, let's see how our moat is.'

The moat was full but its position had been well judged, for the tide was fully in—stopping a few feet from their umbrella and their picnic place—so that they could sit and enjoy their picnic and watch the waves begin to recede, leaving the moat satisfactorily flooded.

The rest of the day passed happily: their picnic, under the shade of the bright beach umbrella as the day grew hotter; in the sea with the children; the feel of the two sturdy little bodies as she helped them to dry and to dress, and on the way home a small sleepy boy on her lap in the car. And Adam saying, when she thanked him for the day, that he had enjoyed it so much and he hoped that they could do it again some time soon.

There had never been a day quite like that before in Julie's life. Somehow she didn't want to begin to think too deeply about why it had been so special. Half-forgotten words kept coming into her mind—'a day of small things'.

And, somehow, because Adam had said what he had and had given up pretending that that night hadn't happened, it seemed to Julie that the last of the barriers between them had fallen.

Not quite the last, perhaps, for although she wanted to ask him about his wife—wanted to say how sorry she was—something stopped her.

But there was no doubt that their working relationship was easier, with no more reservation on Adam's part about her ability to do her job. Julie found that she no longer felt at all defensive; that she could discuss any of the patients, and any concerns she had about them, on equal terms with him.

As she did when Mrs Ngalo was allowed to go home.

'I was checking in my textbook of surgical nursing,' she said to Adam when he was having a quick cup of coffee in her office the day before Mrs Ngalo was to go home. 'The biggest problem when patients leave the hospital situation seems to be trying to do too much too soon—overdoing things and forgetting the way they've been told to move. But somehow I have the feeling that with Mrs Ngalo it's going to be different. She's more likely to do as little as possible in case she does any damage to her hip replacement.'

Adam nodded.

'I think you're right,' he said after a moment. 'She was certainly very nervous about starting to walk, and even since she's been off crutches she never moves without her cane. Which is right at this stage, but not if she lets that go on too long. Tomorrow afternoon she's leaving, isn't she? I should be back from the Clinic by then. I'll have a word with her, and with her husband too.' He put his mug down on the desk and stood up.

'Thanks for your input on that, Sister Maynard.' Formal, professional, but the real warmth of his smile said so much more than the words did. 'And thanks for the coffee—it was a life-saver.'

The following afternoon, soon after Mr Ngalo arrived to take his wife home, Adam joined them in the small room which once again looked impersonal with Mrs Ngalo's family photographs packed away and her suitcase already closed.

'You'll need that cane for a little while, Mrs Ngalo,' Adam said easily, and Julie knew, from the quick glance he had given her, that he had noticed Mrs Ngalo's hand clutching her cane very tightly. 'But as the muscle tone improves, and as you give your hip gentle exercise, what happens is that you're actually re-educating the muscles, and one of the things they have to learn is to manage without the cane.'

'I suppose you're right, Dr Brent,' Mrs Ngalo said doubtfully. 'But what if something goes wrong; what if I fall?'

'If you do, we'll put things right for you again,' Adam said. He leaned forward. 'But you won't fall, Mrs Ngalo. Move around your house slowly, steadily. Do some walking. Walk in the park with these lovely grandchildren of yours. Their pace should be just about right for you. You know you mustn't lift heavy loads and you mustn't do any excessive bending and twisting, but gentle exercise isn't only good—it's necessary. Swimming, now, that's an excellent thing.'

'Now listen to what the doctor is telling you, Mama,' Mr Ngalo said.

Mrs Ngalo, to Julie's surprise and delight, laughed. A rather shaky laugh, but still a laugh.

'Dr Brent, look at me,' she said. 'I have never swum in my life. How could I start now? We don't do that—women in my culture. Oh, the young ones do, but not women my age. And my size.'

Julie looked at the big woman. No, she thought, not swimming for you, Mrs Ngalo.

'See now, Sister Maynard is struggling not to smile,' Mrs Ngalo said. 'No, Dr Brent, I will not be swimming, but I will do the other things you have said.'

They walked along the corridor, Mrs Ngalo using her cane but walking, Julie thought, with more confidence.

'Goodbye, Sister Maynard, and thank you for all you have done for me. Not just looking after me so well, but the way you have talked to me. And thank you, Dr Brent. Perhaps Sister Maynard will let you have one or two of the chocolates in the box I have left for the nurses in my locker.'

They shook hands, and when the lift door had closed Adam looked down at Julie.

'I think she's going to be all right.'

'I think so too,' Julie agreed. 'Even now she was looking more confident.'

A new patient was to be admitted the next day, she knew, but so far all she knew was that this was a lady of seventy who had recently had a stroke.

'Mrs Johnson's condition isn't too good, Sister,' Matron said the next morning when she brought a folder up. 'She has regained her speech, and we'll have a speech therapist in regularly. And, of course, she'll have physiotherapy. But she's had a heart condition for more than ten years, and the stroke has put considerably more strain on her heart.' Her eyes met Julie's.

'I think, really,' she said slowly, 'that her family need

to know that she's being well cared for.'

There was often, Julie was finding, a feeling of guilt among relatives—a feeling that they should be the ones to do the caring and the looking after. Mrs Ngalo had said that her daughters and daughters-in-law felt this very strongly, and it seemed to Julie that this was true of many of the relatives of her patients.

And Mrs Johnson's daughters were no exception.

'We wanted to make things nice for Mum; make her feel at home when she gets here this afternoon,' the younger one explained as they set out photographs and arranged flowers. 'Matron said it would be all right.'

'Of course it is,' Julie assured her. 'We like our patients to feel at home. We're different here at Halvey House because most of our patients are here for longer than a hospital stay. With someone like your mother, our immediate goal is to retrain the affected arm and leg and to help her regain as much independence as possible. And we will, of course, be watching her heart condition.'

The older daughter turned from putting some fruit into a pretty pottery bowl. 'I wanted to give up my job so that we could have Mum at home, Sister,' she said, not quite steadily. 'I'm a teacher. But she was so distressed at the very idea that we had to leave it. And Helen has a lot of running around with her children—it wouldn't have worked.'

'If Dad had still been alive we might have managed,' her sister said. 'He could have been with her when I had to be out. But as it is—'

'We'll look after her for you, and we'll make her feel at home,' Julie said quietly. 'I promise you that. And we're not strict about visiting times, so you can come pretty much when it's possible for you.'

Mrs Johnson arrived by ambulance from the hospital that afternoon. The stroke had affected her right side, leaving her right arm and leg barely mobile. But she smiled when she saw her room, and shook her head.

'You girls,' she said with obvious affection. 'You didn't tell me you were going to do this.'

'Girls, indeed,' her elder daughter, Jane, said, smiling. 'I'm forty-five, and Louise wil be forty on her birthday.'

'You'll always be girls to me,' her mother returned serenely. She turned to Julie. 'How nice of you, Sister, to arrange tea for us. Thank you.'

Julie looked at her new patient, seeing the dark shadows under her eyes. 'When you've had tea I'm going to chase both your girls away, Mrs Johnson,' she said. 'You need to rest.'

A little later, when the two daughters had gone, she and Prudence settled Mrs Johnson. Her right arm was splinted to prevent the muscles from contracting, and Julie positioned a small cushion under the arm.

'That feels much better, Sister, thank you,' Mrs Johnson murmured, her eyelids already drooping.

'She's going to be one of these very undemanding patients, I can see,' Julie said to Prudence when they left. 'Dr Brent will be talking to the physiotherapist but what we have to watch for, because of the heart condition, is shortness of breath, cyanosis, any chest pain and increased pulse rate after that exercise period. I've made a note on her chart of her physio times, and we'll monitor how that goes. We have to find the right balance between helping her to regain mobility and putting any strain on her heart.'

The coming weekend Julie was off duty, and she couldn't help wondering if Adam would suggest the beach again, or perhaps something else. Wondering and, she had to admit, hoping. But he said nothing, and when the young accountant she had met at the party in Camps Bay phoned on Saturday and asked her out she accepted.

It was a pleasant evening—a film and then a pizza at the Waterfront. And his goodnight kiss, too, was pleasant and undemanding.

'Thanks, Richard, it was a lovely evening,' Julie said.

'Can I give you a ring again—maybe next week?' he asked as he left her, and she said, meaning it, that she would like that.

She rose early on Sunday morning to have a swim in the pool before anyone else was around. But just as she was getting out, her hair dripping, Adam and the children came along the path from their cottage.

'Julie, will you watch me swim?' Catherine said eagerly. 'I can even swim in the deep end.'

'And me,' David put in. 'You must see me dive, Julie.'

'I didn't know you'd be here,' Adam said a little awkwardly. He hesitated, but only for a moment. 'I rang you last night, actually, but you were out.'

'Yes, I was at the cinema, and then having a pizza,' Julie said, wondering why she felt she had to explain.

'Nice evening?' Adam asked, very casually.

'Very pleasant,' Julie said, equally casually.

But there must have been something in the way she said it that told him that it had been no more than that. He smiled—a slow, warm smile.

'I'm glad,' he said softly. 'I'm very glad, Julie.'

CHAPTER SIX

JULIE and Adam watched the children in the pool, Catherine swimming carefully and concentrating on her strokes and her breathing, David excited and exuberant.

'Watch me, Daddy. Look how I can turn round, Julie. Now I'm going to swim on my back,' he told them, spluttering as he disappeared under the water. Adam shook his head, smiling.

'If he would cut out the running commentary he'd manage better,' he said.

'I can dive,' David said then proudly, and he clambered out of the pool and did a belly-flop, which splashed Julie and Adam and made Julie wince.

'Oh, dear, did that hurt, David?' she asked, but the small boy shook his head.

'I've been trying to teach him the right way to dive,' Adam said, 'but the real problem is that he doesn't think his own diving leaves anything to be desired. He thinks it's perfect!'

He was a very good swimmer himself, Julie saw a little later as Adam dived in at the deep end and swam a swift and economical crawl up and down the pool, his brown body cutting through the clear blue water.

'You're pretty good,' she said when he was sitting beside her at the edge of the pool, towelling his brown hair.

'I swam for the medical school team,' he told her, 'but that was a long time ago. You're not too bad yourself. We watched you when we arrived.'

'I wasn't swimming seriously,' Julie said. 'Not in this.'

Adam glanced consideringly at her bikini.

'No, I can believe that,' he said, and smiled. 'I must admit I thought you might be in trouble when you did that fast turn just before you came out.'

'Oh,' Julie said a little faintly, remembering that she had almost lost the top of her bikini at that stage.

'I'm hungry,' David said, climbing out of the pool. 'But I don't want my egg mixed up. Lying down or standing up, but not mixed up.'

'All right, son,' Adam replied equably. 'Not scrambled, then.' He turned to Julie. 'In case you haven't worked that out, lying down is fried and standing up is boiled.'

He hesitated.

'Would you like to have breakfast with us, Julie? It will probably turn out to be eggs standing up, for quickness, because I promised my folks we'd go through and visit them—they live in Stellenbosch.'

'I like eggs standing up,' Julie assured him.

The kitchen of the cottage was bright and sunny, and Julie helped Catherine to set out pretty chintz mats on the oak table. It was when Adam got up to put more toast on that Catherine asked if Julie couldn't come with them to see Grandma and Grandpa.

'Thank you, Catherine, but I couldn't do that,' Julie said quickly. 'It's very nice of you, but I'm sure your grandparents are looking forward to the day on their own with you.'

Adam came back to the table with two more slices of toast. 'I was thinking of suggesting that myself, Julie,' he said. 'That's if you haven't any other plans?'

'No, I don't,' Julie admitted. 'Just catching up on some washing and letter-writing, but—'

She watched him spreading toast for David, his big hands careful.

'Daddy does Marmite the nice way,' David explained.

'When Beauty spreads toast for me the Marmite isn't the nice way.'

Adam looked up and smiled. 'I'm not sure,' he said, 'but I think it's because I spread the butter right to the corners first. Soldiers, David?' The little boy nodded.

Inexplicably there was a tightness in Julie's throat as the big doctor carefully cut his small son's toast into fingers. He is a good father, she thought, and it can't have been easy.

Adam stood up. 'I'll ring my mother,' he said briskly. 'She'll be delighted.'

Julie felt doubtful about that, but the thought of spending the day with Adam and the children was too tempting to refuse. And an hour later, when they reached the cottage nestling on the slopes of a vine-covered hill overlooking the beautiful small town and Adam's mother welcomed her, she had to admit that Mrs Brent certainly seemed to be pleased.

'Grandpa's just up the hill with Tess,' she told the children when she had hugged and kissed them. 'Take Shandy and go and meet him.'

The children and the big golden dog ran confidently off along a path that headed up the hill.

'The kettle's on; we'll have tea right away,' she said comfortably. 'Come in, Julie.'

The whitewashed thatched cottage had thick walls, and it was cool inside. Julie looked around her—at the soft colours of the rugs on the wooden floors, the golden glow of the dining-room table and the soft chintz of the chairs and couches.

'What a lovely house,' she exclaimed involuntarily.

Adam's mother looked pleased.

'We love it,' she said. 'When we sold the farm a few years ago we kept the cottage. We'd always planned on living here when George retired.'

She was small and slim, with blue eyes clear in her

suntanned face. A little older than my own mother, Julie thought, but there is something about her that reminds me of Mum. And there was a sudden pang of homesickness at this thought.

Adam was more like his father, she thought when the children came in with their grandfather and a small black and white collie who didn't know whether to greet Adam, or Julie, or concentrate on teasing Shandy.

'Shandy is Tess's boyfriend,' Catherine told Julie seriously. 'She likes him a lot, and he just loves her.' The collie was lying down now, her head resting on her paws as she watched Shandy intently.

'What she really needs,' Adam's father said, 'is a flock of sheep, but she's prepared to round up anything that moves.' He smiled at his small granddaughter. 'Specially if it's her boyfriend, Catherine.'

'It's one of those beautiful platonic friendships,' Adam said, smiling. 'Certainly as far as Tess is concerned, since she's had her operation.'

He looks so much younger, so much more relaxed here, Julie found herself thinking as she looked at Adam's brown head leaning back against the chintz cushion of the big armchair and saw the easiness of his smile.

'It's so hot,' Mrs Brent said, 'that I thought we'd wait and eat later. Catherine—David—Grandpa and I are dying to watch *Fantasia* again. Would you like that?' She turned to Adam. 'I know it's hot but if you go through the wood and up by the dam, most of the path is shady and you get that wonderful view down over the town. I'm sure Julie would enjoy that.'

There was no argument from either of the children, whether because of the attraction of watching *Fantasia* or because—and Julie thought this was it—small as she was, their grandmother made it pretty clear, in a pleasant and firm way, that she didn't expect them to argue.

And nor were the dogs given a choice. 'You've both been out,' she told them when Adam opened the door. 'You'll get out again later when it's cool. Come and lie down through here. Tess! Shandy!'

Obediently, the collie and the Labrador followed her.

'Yes, we all know she's the boss,' Adam agreed when Julie commented, smiling. 'We don't mind, though.'

'My mother is much the same,' Julie told him.

The path through the wood and along the side of the dam was cool and shady. At the far end of the dam the ground fell away, and the small town, looking sleepy in the heat-haze, lay below them.

'Over there,' Adam said, pointing, 'is the stadium where Pavarotti sang last year.'

Julie couldn't see where he was pointing so he moved closer to her and took her hand in his.

'Look,' he said, holding her hand and pointing it. 'Straight across.'

'Were you there?' Julie asked. 'He didn't come to Durban so we didn't get the chance to hear him.'

Adam nodded, his arm still around her shoulders.

'It was wonderful,' he said. 'That incredible voice in the amphitheatre of the hills. The clouds lifted and the sun came through, and a hang-glider appeared from that hill over there and floated over the stadium.'

'It must have been unforgettable,' Julie said, and all at once she was very conscious of his body very close to hers and of his arm around her shoulders. She thought that it might be wise if she moved away but, even as she thought it, she knew that that was the last thing she wanted to do.

'Julie,' Adam said softly.

His kiss was gentle, friendly, undemanding, and the feel of his arms around her, holding her close to him, was very pleasant. Just a kiss, Julie thought, a little dazed by the heat of the day and the beauty of this place. Just a kiss, that's all.

She wasn't sure, afterwards, when something had changed. But Adam's lips were searching, demanding, and once again everything in her responded to the urgency of his body so close to hers. The grass was warm underneath her, and the sun—shining through the trees—was dappled. She closed her eyes, and there was nothing else in the world but the two of them—this man, and herself.

Later—much later—he looked down at her.

'Julie—' he began.

She put one finger over his lips.

'Don't say it,' she told him, not quite steadily. 'Don't say you're sorry.'

He smiled.

'I wasn't going to,' he replied. 'But—I don't want you to think I brought you here with this in mind.'

'Why not?' Julie said, surprising herself a little. 'I can't think of a more wonderful place.'

He laughed, his head thrown back. And then, the laughter gone, his eyes met hers.

'When I kissed you,' he said slowly, 'it was just going to be a, well, just a friendly sort of kiss—because you're a pretty girl, because we're in this lovely place, because I know I wasn't particularly welcoming when you came to Halvey House, because—Anyway, that kiss kind of got out of hand.' His grey eyes darkened.

'But I don't have to tell you that,' he said, and Julie felt her cheeks grow warm.

'No, you don't,' she agreed, and she knew that her voice was less than steady. 'But you know what the song says, Adam—it takes two to tango, and I wasn't exactly fighting you off.' The laughter was back in his eyes.

'No,' he said solemnly. 'No, I wouldn't say you were doing that.'

Julie put her hand over his.

'It's all right, Adam,' she said softly, meaning it. 'We don't have to get all heavy and introspective. We— seem to find this physical attraction thing a bit strong, that's all.'

All?

She knew, as she said it, that she was playing down a feeling which was stronger than anything she had ever known. But something told her that this could be more than Adam could handle right now. So making light of it seemed a good idea.

'You were right, though,' she said, 'you weren't too welcoming.'

It was a moment before he replied.

'I know,' he said. And then, shrugging, continued, 'I did judge you much too quickly, without giving you a chance. Look, Julie, it was unforgivable, but I've seen young pretty girls decide they want to do something but it doesn't turn out to be what they expected and they quit. That is so bad for our folks in Halvey House— they need security, they need commitment. They don't need to become fond of someone, and then have her go away.'

Julie waited, sensing that there was more he wanted to say.

There was a bleakness about his face that shook her, a remoteness that made him far removed from the man who had just held her in his arms.

'I'm not going to do that, Adam,' she said steadily after a little while. 'I'm not saying I'll spend the rest of my life working at Halvey House, but I'm certainly not going to walk away now or in the near future.'

She wanted to say, Come back to me; come back from wherever you are. But he was a stranger again—

this man with the darkness in his eyes, with the bleak line of his jaw.

'Julie,' he said slowly, and he was back with her, looking down at her almost, she thought, as if he was making his mind up about something. Or trying to.

But the next moment, with an effort, he smiled.

'You're right,' he said, and he took both her hands in his. 'I believe you, and I'll stop worrying about my patients losing their Sister Sunshine. Come on—time we were getting back.'

He swung her hand lightly in his as they walked back along the side of the dam and through the vineyards and the wood.

Whatever Adam had been going to say, he had changed his mind. He had put it behind him, and Julie had to accept that. But she had the strong feeling that, whatever it was, it needed to be said and she would just have to wait for him to do that.

His mother was busy in the kitchen when they got back to the cottage, and they could hear sounds of laughter from the room next door.

'I think your dad enjoys the "Dance of the Hours" as much as Catherine and David do,' Mrs Brent said, smiling, as she took a chicken pie out of the oven. 'He loves the bit with the hippopotamus sleeping—so do I!'

She handed a large bowl of salad to Julie. 'Put this on the table out on the stoep, will you, Julie?'

When Julie came back to the kitchen Mrs Brent said, 'Isn't it beautiful up there beside the dam? I love the view down over the valley, and it's always so quiet and so peaceful.'

'Yes, it is beautiful,' Julie agreed. For a moment her eyes met Adam's, and she could feel the tell-tale warmth in her cheeks at their shared memory.

'Good, that sounds like the end of *Fantasia*,' Mrs Brent said. 'Adam, tell them we're ready to eat, please.'

It was a noisy and happy family meal, although Julie could see that both Mr and Mrs Brent could be firm with the children when necessary. As Adam himself was, she knew.

'Time to head back,' Adam said at last with regret. 'School tomorrow for you two, and work for me and for Julie.'

'But not for Shandy, and not for Tess,' David said. 'And not for you, Grandpa, since you're retired.' He thought for a moment and then said thoughtfully, his copper head on one side, 'I think maybe I'll retire from playschool.'

'Nonsense,' his grandmother said briskly. 'You love playschool. Haven't you just been telling Grandpa and I all the things you do there?'

'Yes, I do like it,' the little boy agreed, 'but if I retired then we could stay here later, and I do like being here.'

Mrs Brent kissed the top of his head. 'You'll come again soon, David,' she said. Across the table, she smiled at Julie. 'And I hope you will too, Julie.'

'I'd like that,' Julie said, meaning it.

It was dark when Adam drew up outside his cottage.

'Look, Table Mountain is all bright,' Catherine said sleepily.

'They put floodlights on the mountain for the whole summer,' her father said. He looked at Julie. 'Have you been up the mountain yet, Julie? No? I've been promising the children we'd do that some time—not necessarily at night, though. Daytime might be better, when you can see the whole peninsula. Maybe we can do it some weekend when you're off?'

Julie's heart turned over. Whatever the shadow and the reserve had been, all that was gone and he was talking about their—friendship? She hesitated over the word, but even in her thoughts it seemed better to settle for that—yes, friendship as something ongoing.

'Yes, I'd like that,' she said.

At the children's insistence, she helped to bath them and put them to bed. David was almost asleep before she and Adam left the room, Catherine sleepily insisting that she wanted to read for a little while.

They didn't talk about their mother much, she thought when she had kissed both the children goodnight. Catherine did occasionally, but she hadn't heard David mention her at all. Almost two years—it was a long time, of course, in their short lives.

'I'll walk to the corner with you,' Adam said when Julie made a move to go. He hadn't suggested that she stayed longer, and somehow that seemed right—there had been enough already in this day. Perhaps it was better for each of them to be on their own now. Not that Adam was on his own, of course, with his children asleep close to him.

'Goodnight, Julie,' he said softly when they parted. In the warm darkness, she could feel him looking down at her. Then, very gently, his lips brushed hers.

'Goodnight,' he said again.

It was a very different kiss from his kiss on the mountain. But Julie found herself smiling as she left him.

Mrs Smit's daughter-in-law, Rietta, had been to visit the day before, Julie discovered the next morning. Her heart sank because she was determined to find the chance to talk to her.

'I'm sorry I missed her,' she said when she was checking Mrs Smit's pulse and blood pressure.

'She'll be back this afternoon,' Mrs Smit told her. She looked at the chart in Julie's hand. 'I feel a fraud, Sister. I don't really need to be looked after now.'

'You still need your daily physio,' Julie reminded her.

'But not for much longer,' the older woman said. She

looked at Julie. 'Rietta brought more clothes for me, for when I go to stay with my brother and his wife. She—didn't say how long they think I should stay before I go back to the farm.'

That afternoon Julie caught Rietta Smit as she came out of the lift, and asked if they could have a talk in her office.

'She's all right, isn't she, my mother-in-law?' the young woman asked.

'Yes, she's doing very well,' Julie replied. She hesitated. It wasn't easy because she didn't know the best way to go about this, but perhaps head-on was best.

'Mrs Smit—Rietta,' she said slowly, 'your mother-in-law would much rather come home to the farm than go to her brother.'

'She hasn't said that,' Rietta said, surprised. 'I thought she'd quite enjoy a few weeks in town with Johan and Nell.'

'She misses the children and the dogs and, well, she just misses the farm,' Julie told her.

Rietta looked down at her clasped hands.

'She's never said that.' Her voice was low. 'I sometimes think the children are a bit noisy, and—and I'm never sure that she's happy about the way I do things. She ran the farm so efficiently all those years, especially after Pieter's father died, that I can't help feeling she thinks I don't do as good a job.' Julie looked at her.

'Would you mind if she came home right away?' she said.

'Mind? No, I'd be pleased. The children miss her, and I like knowing she's there in her cottage close to us.' For a moment her blue eyes were filled with tears. 'I miss my own mother—my folks are in the Free State—and even if we're not as close as I'd hoped we'd be, it's good to know she's there. But I do worry about the children being a nuisance.'

Julie stood up.

'Come on, Rietta,' she said briskly. 'It seems to me there's been enough pussyfooting around.'

Looking decidedly nervous, Rietta followed her along the corridor.

'Mrs Smit,' Julie said, 'I've just been telling Rietta that what you'd really like is to go home as soon as possible. I've told her, too, how much you miss the children.' She looked at Rietta.

'Is that right, Mother Smit?' the younger woman said—a little nervously, Julie could hear, but at least she was saying it.

'Yes, I do miss them,' her mother-in-law said. 'And I miss the dogs, and I miss just being on the farm— being near you and Pieter.'

Rietta sat down. 'I sometimes think,' she said slowly, 'that you feel I don't run things very well.' Mrs Smit shook her head.

'I'm sorry if you feel that, because I think you do a good job. It isn't easy, running the house and helping with the farm accounts. I know that. I remember when we were first married I used to dread Piet checking my Egg Book and my Chicken Book. You have computers now, of course.'

'And, believe me, that makes it even more difficult,' Rietta said fervently.

She smiled, and her mother-in-law smiled back. There was some way to go but it was a start, and a good enough start. Julie left them to it and, as she walked back along the corridor, she was smiling too.

Adam was waiting in her office.

'You look pleased with yourself, Sister,' he said.

'I am pleased with myself,' Julie replied.

She told him about Mrs Smit and her daughter-in-law.

'Well done,' Adam said, and he smiled. 'Well done, Sister.'

It's all right, Julie thought thankfully. Nothing that had happened yesterday had made any difference to this new, easy working relationship between Adam and her. Nothing that had happened, and nothing that he had said.

Although she couldn't help feeling that perhaps whatever it was that he hadn't said was more important.

Julie was worried about Ted Ramsay, her multiple sclerosis patient.

There was always a danger, she knew, of a flare-up of his disease, and so many different things might set that off. A cold, an infection, an emotional upset—the last one, she was confident, wouldn't happen with Ted for Linda, his wife, was supportive and somehow always managed to be pleasant and serene, keeping her concerns to herself—certainly while she was with her husband.

But there had been a few colds among the other patients and, although Ted Ramsay's symptoms were slight, Julie began to notice a further lack of co-ordination and then an increased wrist tremor.

'Yes, I've been watching it too,' Adam said when she mentioned it to him. 'I've brought something to try out. I don't know if they will help, but anything is worth trying. Weighted wrist cuffs. It should give the wrist a little more stability.'

They went along to Ted's room, and Adam fitted the wrist cuffs onto the man's thin wrists.

'Well, now,' Ted said, and Julie's heart ached at his ability to manage a smile. 'Here I am thinking I'd led a pretty blameless life, and you're putting handcuffs on me!' Adam sat down on the edge of the bed.

'I think,' he said casually, 'we'll skip the physio for a few days. Just until you're over this touch of a cold.' He turned to Julie. 'We'll have a look at Ted's medication, too, Sister.'

Back in the office, he held Ted's chart in his hands.

'We'll risk stepping up the muscle-relaxant drug,' he said after a moment, 'because we must try to reduce that spasticity. I don't like stopping his physio—even for a few days—because the muscle power is diminishing fast. But the risk of extreme fatigue is too great.' He put the chart down.

'What really worries me,' he said slowly, 'is his breathing. He's had chest problems right from the start, and even a slight cold could make that so much worse.'

At the door, he turned. 'Let me know immediately if there are any side-effects from the increased muscle-relaxant drugs, Sister.'

Later, at the end of visiting time, Ted's wife, Linda, knocked on the door of Julie's office.

'Can I come in, Sister?' she said.

'Of course,' Julie said. 'Sit down, Mrs Ramsay.'

The older woman sat down. In the clear light from the window behind, Julie could see signs of strain on her face.

'Ted's got quite a bit worse in the last little while, Sister,' she said quietly. There was no use denying that.

'Yes, he has,' Julie replied. 'It is a progressive disease, Mrs Ramsay. You know that.'

Mrs Ramsay nodded. 'Yes, I know.' Her voice was low. 'But, even with these things on his wrist, he can't hold a cup now and he used to be able to do that. Will he be able to do that again in a little while?'

Julie knew that Adam felt that both Ted and his wife needed and deserved honesty. 'No, Mrs Ramsay,' she said steadily. 'With multiple sclerosis, once certain abilities have been lost they are almost impossible to regain.'

Linda Ramsay sat for a long time without saying anything. Then she looked at Julie and smiled.

'Well, I held his cup for him today, and I can just go on doing that. He says if we spill it between us maybe

I'd better get the feeding-cup we have for our little Natasha, so we had a laugh about that.' She stood up.

'You don't need to pinch Natasha's cup,' Julie said, and she managed to match the other woman's lightness. 'I'd been thinking it was time to give Ted a feeding-cup with a spout for easiness.'

She walked along with Mrs Ramsay to the lift, and just before she said goodbye she mentioned quietly that Dr Brent was a little worried about Ted's breathing.

'But we're watching him very carefully, Mrs Ramsay,' she said. Linda Ramsay nodded.

'I know.' Her brown eyes met Julie's. 'When Ted first came in here, Sister, I hated the thought of having to let him be looked after by anyone but me. But our doctor had said we couldn't go on, having him at home, so I agreed. I've never regretted it. He's happy here and he doesn't worry now about it all being too much for me, getting him in and out of the chair and helping him to bath. So—so when you say you're watching him carefully I know I can trust you—you and Dr Brent, and the others here.'

Julie was very glad that she had mentioned their concern about Ted's breathing to his wife because two days later she had to phone the Clinic to ask Dr Brent to call her as soon as he came out of Theatre.

'It's Ted Ramsay, Dr Brent,' she said when he phoned half an hour later. 'His breathing has become considerably worse.'

'I'll skip the couple of visits I was going to do here, and I'll come right away,' Adam replied.

Julie knew that she was right to send for him, and the tightening of his jaw as he examined Ted Ramsay confirmed that. For a moment his eyes met hers.

'We're going to have to get some help on this, Ted,' he said. 'I'm going to arrange for you to go to hospital. You need to be on a ventilator to help you to breathe.'

'Can't you do that for me here, Dr Brent?' Ted asked with difficulty. Adam shook his head.

'We're not equipped to do that, I'm afraid,' he said. 'I'm going to arrange for you to be taken to Groote Schuur. You'll be in Intensive Care, Ted, so that the machine can be properly monitored.'

Ted looked at Julie. 'Could you phone Linda and let her know?' he asked, and Julie said that she would. When the hospital arrangements had been made Julie phoned Ted's wife.

'I'll come right away,' Linda Ramsay said. 'Can I go in the ambulance with him?' When Adam had confirmed that she could do that Julie put the phone down.

'He'll have to be heavily sedated on the ventilator,' Adam said. 'I'll tell his wife.'

Julie knew the reason from textbooks, and from her brief experience in Intensive Care after she'd qualified, and she was impressed by Adam's brief explanation to Linda Ramsay while they waited for the ambulance.

'The reason for keeping him heavily sedated,' he said, 'is because his own breathing could get out of synch with the ventilator, and if that happens his body would instinctively fight the machine. So we have to hand over, and let the ventilator do the work until Ted's lungs can take over again.'

Linda Ramsay's voice was controlled and even, but her hands were clasped very tightly.

'When you say ''heavily sedated'', Dr Brent,' she asked, quietly, 'how heavily do you mean?'

'I mean so heavily that when you visit him he won't know you're there, Mrs Ramsay,' Adam said. 'That's necessary, I'm afraid.'

After a moment Linda Ramsay managed a small smile. 'I don't think Ted would like that whole Intensive Care scene,' she said, and her voice was very steady, 'so it's just as well he won't know much about it.'

She stood up. 'I'll go back to him now.'

The ambulance came ten minutes later, and Adam went off in his own car to see his patient settled. Julie was just going off duty when he came back.

'I took Mrs Ramsay home,' he said, coming into the office. 'Her car is here, but she'll get a lift and pick it up tomorrow.'

'How is Ted?' Julie asked.

'They were still stabilising him,' Adam said. 'Takes some time, and it isn't helped in Ted's case by the nature of his illness. The ICU staff are good—they have to be. But they have to be ready to suction, to use a hand-ventilator if necessary, to check that there is adequate humidification, to measure the oxygen concentration— you know all this, Julie.'

Julie knew, too, that getting a patient off the ventilator, when the need for it was over, could be the hardest part for the skilled staff at the big hospital.

'I'm glad you sent for me when you did,' Adam said as he left. 'We got him before that breathing became a real emergency.'

Ted Ramsay was such a quiet man and so unde-manding that Julie was surprised at the difference his absence made. Not only to her, and to the rest of the staff, but to the other patients.

'Going to be all right, is he, Sister?' Captain O'Connor asked gruffly. 'Good fellow, Ted.'

'Poor Mr Ramsay,' Miss Clifford said, shaking her head. 'He always had a smile for us all, no matter how he was feeling.'

'How is Mrs Ramsay?' Mrs Smit asked. 'Things are difficult enough for her anyway, without the worry of this.'

Julie reassured them all as best she could. And each day Adam phoned for a report on Ted's condition. It was a week before the doctor in charge felt that he could begin to wean Ted from the ventilator.

'If that goes well another week could see Ted back,' Adam told Julie. 'And although he's still sedated they ease the sedation in the times he's off the ventilator. His wife was there when I looked in today—she said he was very drowsy but he had recognised her.'

'That must have helped her,' Julie said. She looked at him and said, without giving herself time to think, 'You look tired, Dr Brent.'

'I am tired, Sister Maynard,' Adam replied, and he smiled. 'An emergency op at the Clinic at two o'clock this morning. I just got back in time to take the kids to school.'

'What do you do when you have to go out in the middle of the night like that?' Julie asked. 'With Catherine and David, I mean.'

'Beauty lives in the staff quarters close by,' Adam said. 'I phone her, and she comes right away. It—isn't ideal, but it works.'

He smiled. 'Anyway, it's half-term, and my folks are coming through this morning to take the kids back with them for a couple of days. So I'll have an early night tonight, and hope there are no more emergencies.' He stood up.

'With the weather this hot, I plan on having a swim around nine o'clock tonight. No one else ever uses the pool at night. I—was wondering if you might like to do that too?'

'I might,' Julie said, and she hoped that she sounded as casual as Adam had. Because this was the first time that he had suggested meeting her without the children.

Later she began to wonder if it really was a good idea. She had always prided herself on being realistic— on facing up to things. And there was no denying this chemistry between herself and Adam. It was strange, peculiar, unexpected, because he wasn't the sort of man she usually fell for.

Not that she had fallen for him, she told herself, swiftly rearranging her thoughts. No, it was just a little disturbing, the way she felt close to him. So perhaps it would be wise just to avoid being alone with him. Yes, she was sure that was the way to handle it.

In spite of these thoughts she went out of Halvey House and along the path to the pool just after nine that night, with her towelling robe over her bathing costume and her big bright towel over her arm.

The pool was in darkness, but she could hear the steady, rhythmic sound of someone swimming. There was just enough moonlight, as she got closer, for her to see Adam as he reached the deep end and stopped.

'Lights don't seem to be working,' he told her a little breathlessly, 'but the water is lovely.'

In the warm darkness the water felt wonderful. Like silk, Julie thought as she got in. Warm silk. She swam the ten lengths that was her minimum, with Adam swimming on the other side of the pool. He was out before she was, his towel round him and his hair already rubbed dry.

'You're lucky,' Julie said, her voice muffled as she towelled her hair. 'This mop takes ages to dry.'

Without a word, Adam took her towel from her, and rubbed her hair gently but firmly.

'Thanks, Adam,' Julie said, all at once a little awkward. 'You're good at that.' She could hear in his voice that he was smiling.

'I'm used to drying Catherine's hair,' he reminded her. In the darkness he touched her hair gently. 'There isn't as much of it, of course. You're not quite dry, but you probably like to do something with it before it's completely dry?'

She answered the question in his voice. 'I comb it,

that's all,' she said, 'but I've forgotten to bring
my comb.'

'Come and have a cup of coffee at the cottage,' Adam
said. 'You can comb your hair there.'

Julie hesitated, all her earlier doubts returning. And
not without reason, she knew, for she could feel her
heart thudding unevenly and all her senses were very
much aware of the man beside her, the man whose strong
hands had just dried her hair.

'Julie,' Adam said, very gently, 'I'll behave.'

Afterwards she went hot and cold when she
remembered her reply, but she said it without giving
herself a moment to think.

'You might, I'm not so sure if I will,' she said.

There was a moment's astonished silence and then
Adam burst out laughing, his brown head thrown back.

'Julie—Sister Sunshine—you are priceless!' he said
at last. He took her hand.

'One cup of coffee, and we will both be models of
propriety,' he said, and the laughter was still in his voice.

He led the way along the path back to his cottage,
sure-footed himself, but when Julie stumbled he took
her hand. The cottage was quiet as Shandy had gone
with the children, he told her.

'Kettle's on—we'll sit down while it boils,' he said.

They talked for a little about Ted Ramsay, and the
slow but steady progress he was making. Then Julie saw
that Adam's eyelids were drooping.

'I'll make the coffee,' she said, standing up. 'I know
where everything is—Catherine showed me.'

It was a strange feeling to be in this kitchen on her
own, she thought, without the children here and with
Adam in the next room. And she thought, her cheeks
warm, How could I have said what I did?

She put the two mugs of coffee on a tray, knowing
that Adam liked one spoonful of sugar in his. But when

she carried the tray through she stopped. He was asleep, his head back on the cushion.

She stood looking at him and then, quietly, she put the tray down on the coffee-table and sat down in the chair opposite him.

He was so different from any other man she had known, she thought. He wasn't the tall, dark and handsome sort of fellow that Tim Curran and Mark Elliott both were—Tim with his Sean Connery smile, and Mark with those incredible blue eyes and that cleft in his chin. No, Adam was—a very ordinary man, with his brown hair and his grey eyes.

But she had seen those competent brown hands carefully pour milky tea for a little girl to drink; she had seen them help a small boy to build a sandcastle. Not to mention seeing them competent and professional in caring for an old person.

And there was another memory. Adam's hands on her back, smoothing in suntan lotion at the beach that day. Adam's hands, and the way she had felt. There is more to the way I feel about him, Julie thought slowly, reluctantly. More than that disturbing physical attraction.

In a way it was something of a relief to admit this to herself, knowing as she did so that this knowledge had been slowly creeping to the surface of her consciousness. But this was a man who had lost his wife, she reminded herself. If—and just if—he felt anything like this too he must need time to come to terms with that.

She smiled, for there would be time. Time for her, and time for Adam, too, to get used to this strange new feeling. To let the slow and almost unwilling friendship between them grow at the same time as this disturbing attraction.

Adam opened his eyes. 'Julie, I'm sorry,' he said, sitting up. 'That was unforgivable.' Julie smiled.

'Don't worry,' she said. 'The coffee is just at the right drinking temperature now.'

She put his mug of coffee down beside him. When she had done that he put up one hand and touched her hair.

'Combed and dry,' he murmured, his voice still sleepy. 'And so pretty. Catherine says you have hair like a fairy princess.'

And, in spite of the things she had said and he had said, he took her in his arms, drawing her down close to him. His lips were warm on hers and his arms held her close, so close that she didn't know whether it was his heart or her own which was thudding unevenly.

But he was holding back, she knew, and with difficulty she managed to control her instinctive response to his nearness. After a while he released her gently.

'Julie,' he said, his voice troubled, 'there's something I have to say to you.' As she had done once before, she put one finger over his lips.

'It's all right, Adam,' she said softly. 'I know it must be difficult for you—whatever is happening between us—after losing your wife. This time without her must have been so awful for you. I understand that.'

He drew back, and sat up very straight.

'No, you don't understand,' he said, and there was something in his voice that made her look at him, startled. 'You don't understand at all, Julie.' He looked at her, his grey eyes very dark.

'You know, I suppose, that my wife was killed in a car accident,' he said evenly. 'What you don't know— what very few people know—is that when it happened she was leaving me. Leaving me, leaving the children. She was going away with someone else.'

It was a moment before Julie could speak.

'Oh, Adam,' she said unsteadily. 'Oh, Adam, I'm so sorry.'

She wanted to put her arms around him, to hold him close, but there was something so closed, so remote in his face that she knew she couldn't do that.

All she could do, right now, was sit here and wait for him to go on, with her heart aching for the hurt she could see in his face.

CHAPTER SEVEN

'I WANTED you to know, Julie,' Adam said at last quietly. And then, his eyes steady on hers, he went on, 'You have to know—the way things are with us.'

Julie hesitated, but only for a moment. 'How are things with us, Adam?' she asked him. He smiled, but the smile didn't quite reach his eyes.

'Do we have to spell that out?' he said, and added, 'Perhaps we do. You know how we started off, and that was my fault. I looked at you, and I saw another Celia. Oh, you're not like her to look at, but I suppose I thought, she's young, she's pretty, she can't possibly be committed to working in an old-age home. She'll stay for a while, people will get fond of her and then she'll walk away. Just as Celia did. Or just as she was going to do. Because I had known for months that she was going. I just didn't know when.'

His face was bleak with the memory, and Julie moved closer to him and put her hand on his. After a moment he covered it with his other hand, and now the bleakness had left his eyes.

'And then I was completely thrown by the way I felt about you. I was so sure I knew the sort of girl you were and I didn't need someone like you in my working life, let alone in my private life. That night, when you came back late and that fellow kissed you, I thought that confirmed everything I had thought about you— justified all my doubts. But then you did so many things that made me realise I hadn't given you a chance. You mended Catherine's teddy for her, and you tied a bow on him. You were so good, so professional with our patients and, at the same time, more than that. And with Catherine and David—even with Shandy.'

Gently, with one finger, he touched her lips. 'And then,' he said softly, 'there was that day beside the dam.'

Oh, yes, Julie thought, yes, Adam, there was that day.

'I knew then that I had to tell you about Celia,' he said, and his voice was steady. 'Because—Julie, this is not easy to say, and I don't want to hurt you. You are becoming much too important to me, and to the children, and I'm not sure that I can handle that. I know you are very different from Celia. I know you're not going to let me or anyone else down—but I'm not too good at trusting people, Julie. I back off, I know that.' His hand left hers, and he sat up very straight.

'I'm not surprised that you do, Adam,' Julie said after a moment. She looked up at him, hoping that she was saying the right thing. 'Is it that you feel things are moving too quickly?'

She had thought, as she watched him sleeping, that he needed more time and she hadn't even known, then, the truth about what had happened to him.

He thought about what she'd said.

'Perhaps I do,' he said slowly. 'It's not only myself I'm thinking about, Julie. The children love you but I don't know how they'd feel about—something more permanent.'

Julie took a deep breath. 'What do you want to do?' she asked him. 'About us?'

Unexpectedly, he smiled.

'I don't think I'd better say what I'd like to do right now,' he said. Julie felt her cheeks grow warm.

'You're blushing,' Adam said and, very gently, he put one hand against her cheek. 'I like that.

'I want to go on seeing you,' he went on. 'I want us to do things together—with the children. And I want us to be on our own sometimes, just the two of us.'

He took both her hands in his. 'Can we do it like that, Julie? Can we take it slowly? I feel I'm being very unfair to you.' She shook her head.

'No, you're being honest,' she said, meaning it. 'Perhaps I need that too, Adam, to take things slowly.' Because now that they had got this far, further than she had got in her own thoughts, there was something else that she would have to think about.

The children. Catherine and David.

Already she was fond of them, and enjoyed being with them. But to reach the point of taking on someone else's children, of accepting them as part of the package deal? I would have to be very sure, very certain, Julie thought, and it was a disturbing thought.

'Yes, you're right,' she said decisively. 'We do need to take things slowly, Adam. We both need time.' His hands tightened on hers.

'I am so glad I've told you all this, Julie,' he said and he smiled, the strain and the weariness gone. 'Come on, it's late. I'll walk you back down to the house.' But he made no move to rise from the couch they were sitting on. After a moment he touched her hair.

'Quite dry now,' he said, and all at once his voice was uneven.

Julie was never sure whether he took her in his arms or whether she moved closer to him, but his lips were on hers, searching, demanding, and now there was no holding back her own response as everything in her body answered the urgency of his.

It was a long time before they drew apart.

'I don't call this taking things slowly,' Julie murmured, not quite steadily.

'No, I'm afraid not,' Adam agreed, quite unrepentant. 'Do you mind?'

'Do you need to ask?' Julie returned.

Adam stood up, and drew her to her feet.

'I am taking you back to the safety of Halvey House,' he told her firmly, but he smiled as he said it. 'Right now.'

A few days later Ted Ramsay was discharged from the hospital, and brought back by ambulance. He was a little thinner, Julie thought, and a little more frail, but undaunted.

'Glad to see you back, Ted. Not a pleasant experience, I'm sure, being on that machine,' Captain O'Connor said gruffly, wheeling himself into Ted's room half an hour after Julie and Prudence had got Ted settled.

'Not pleasant, Captain,' Ted agreed, 'but quite acceptable when you consider the alternative—not breathing at all.'

The old Irishman laughed. 'You're right there,' he agreed.

'In any case,' Ted Ramsay said, 'I didn't know much about it, they had me so heavily sedated. It was only after a week, I think, when they began to get me off the ventilator for short periods that I even knew Linda was there.'

'She was there most of the time, Ted,' Julie said.

'Yes, they told me that. Nice girls in that ICU, and good at their job, but I'm glad to be back here,' he said, looking around his room with satisfaction at the family photographs set out on his dresser, the woollen rug over the back of the chair and the flowers his daughter had brought that morning.

'I think you'd better let Ted rest now, Captain O'Connor,' Julie said firmly, seeing the captain ready to settle down for a good visit. 'No more visitors today, Ted, until your wife comes this evening.' But she relented late that afternoon to allow Mrs Smit to come in to say goodbye.

'So you're off back to the farm, then?' Ted said.

Mrs Smit nodded. 'Yes, we're going right back. I have my exercises to do at home, and there are some that Rietta is going to help me with so I don't have to see a phsyiotherapist. She's coming to pick me up now—three hours and we'll be home.' She held out her hand, and took Ted's hand in hers.

'You look after yourself,' she said, 'and that nice wife of yours. Tell her I'll send her that fruit cake recipe we were talking about.'

Julie went out with her, closing the door behind them. Mrs Smit was walking slowly, but steadily and confidently, she was glad to see.

'Come and see us when you're back in town for your check-up,' she said as the older woman looked around her room, checking that she was ready to go.

'I'll do that,' Mrs Smit said. She looked at her watch. 'Rietta will be here any minute. I'll just say goodbye to Captain O'Connor and to Miss Clifford.'

Miss Clifford and the captain were in the small lounge, playing Scrabble, the two wheelchairs drawn up on each side of the table.

'Sure and the days will not be so bright with you gone, Mrs Smit,' the old Irishman said gallantly. 'We'll be missing you, will we not, Miss Clifford?'

'We certainly will, Captain,' Miss Clifford agreed, but her cheeks were pink and she didn't look too forlorn at the thought, Julie saw with amusement.

'I'll certainly miss the company here,' Mrs Smit said, 'but I'll be kept busy with my grandchildren coming in and out. Rietta wants me to teach Elize to crochet.'

She shook hands with Miss Clifford, and held out her hand to Captain O'Connor. And then, instead of taking his outstretched hand, she bent and kissed him on the cheek, before turning and going out quickly.

'Well I never!' little Miss Clifford said primly. 'That was a little forward of her.'

'Maybe that,' the old man agreed, and he smiled. 'But pleasant, very pleasant. Your turn to play, I think, Miss Clifford.'

Julie left them to it, and followed Mrs Smit back to her room—to find that her daughter-in-law had just arrived.

'Time we were on our way, Mother,' Rietta said briskly. She looked at Julie. 'Three hours in the car— we should have a break, shouldn't we?'

Julie nodded. 'If you could stop every hour, and just let Mrs Smit stretch and walk around, that would be a good idea.'

She walked to the lift with them.

'Goodbye, my dear,' Mrs Smit said. 'And thank you for—for everything.'

And that, Julie couldn't help thinking with satisfaction, was a very happy and positive way to see a patient leaving them.

But she had a strong sense that another patient would leave them soon too, and in a different way. The very nature of Halvey House meant that this was more likely than in any other branch of nursing she had done, and there had been cause for concern about Mrs Johnson, her newest patient, from the time she'd been admitted.

The stroke, in itself, was manageable, and already they had made considerable progress in mobilising her. But the real trouble was the heart condition she had had for the past ten years, undoubtedly made worse by the stroke.

'She has her nitroglycerin tablets and over the years, since the angina was first diagnosed, she's done all the right things and she's only had to use them a few times,' Adam had said when Julie and he were discussing Mrs Johnson. 'We're going very cautiously with physiotherapy for her, and yet she should be helped to become more mobile as soon as possible.

'Tony Morton—he's her cardiac man—doesn't want to change her betablock medication, but he would like her blood pressure and her heart rate checked every four hours. Any drop in that blood pressure, ring him immediately. Don't wait to do it through me.'

A few days after that conversation Julie took a letter, which had just arrived, along to Mrs Johnson's room. Her two daughters were there, Jane on her way home from the school at which she taught and Louise on her way to pick her son up from sports. Julie, her hand on the doorhandle, paused.

'You mustn't think like that, Mum,' Louise was saying, distress in her voice.

'But I just want you both to know that I've left that list. Jane, you're to have my diamond engagement ring, and Louise the gold chain. And I'd like—'

'Please, Mum, stop.' That was Jane. 'You're doing fine. Dr Brent and Dr Morton say you are, and—and you mustn't talk like that; you mustn't think that way. You don't know how much it upsets us to hear you saying things like that.'

Julie heard Mrs Johnson sigh. She pushed the door open. 'A letter for you, Mrs Johnson,' she said. 'Airmail—will it be from your sister in England?'

'Yes, it is,' the old lady said, her voice brighter. 'Alice writes so faithfully. Open it for me, will you, Jane?'

Julie went back to her office, the conversation she'd overheard on her mind. She had been reading as many articles as she could in her nursing journal about the care of old people, and what she had just heard struck a chord. When she heard Mrs Johnson's daughters, coming along towards the lift, she made up her mind.

'Could you come in for a moment?' she asked them. 'I know you're in a hurry but it won't take long.'

There was no easy way to do this, she knew, for her or

for these two women who so clearly loved their mother dearly. She told them quietly that she had overheard their conversation with their mother.

'She mustn't say things like that,' Louise said unsteadily. 'We don't want her jewellery. We—we just want her here.'

'She knows that, I'm sure,' Julie said, her voice gentle. 'And we're all hoping she's going to come through this. But she's not being morbid, you know, wanting to discuss things like this.' She thought for a moment. 'In a way,' she said, slowly, 'it's like a house-wife doing her spring-cleaning. Your mother wants to make these arrangements—to have these discussions— and I think she'll feel better if you allow her to do that.'

Jane, the elder daughter, lifted her head and looked at Julie.

'I don't know if we could manage that,' she said slowly. 'Not without getting upset.'

Julie leaned forward. 'You were saying, both of you, that you wish you could do more for your mother,' she said. 'This is something you really can do. You can help her by letting her say these things, discuss what she wants done, in a matter-of-fact and practical way. It will lift a real load from her shoulders, I'm certain of that.'

The two sisters looked at each other.

'If you think it will help Mum,' Louise said at last, and Jane nodded.

'I'm certain it will,' Julie replied. 'Don't make a big deal of it, but the next time she wants to discuss that sort of thing, let her.'

There wasn't anything more she could do, she thought when they had gone, but she hoped that she had got through to them as she was certain that it would help Mrs Johnson. Whether or not she was going to recover, she was being realistic about her condition and she clearly wanted to face up to it. And, perhaps, help her daughters to do the same.

That weekend she and Adam and the children took Shandy for a walk on the lower slopes of Table Mountain among the pine trees, and she told Adam what she had said to Mrs Johnson's daughters.

'I didn't manage to see them on any of the other days they were in,' she said, 'but Mrs Johnson is less stressed, more relaxed. I think it got through to them.'

'I'm glad you did that,' Adam said. 'Look, she may well pull through, but I'm not happy about her heart and neither is Tony Morton. Anything that takes pressure off her is helpful. I've noticed that some old people have a very serene approach and attitude to death. And you're right, it isn't morbid in any way—it's actually quite practical.'

Catherine and David came running back at that moment, with the big golden dog beside them.

'Can we have our apples now, Daddy?' Catherine asked breathlessly.

'Did we bring any sweeties?' David looked hopeful.

'Yes, to the apples,' Adam said, smiling. 'And, no, David, you know we don't usually bring sweets when we go for walks. Apples are much nicer.'

David shook his head. 'Not to me,' he said mournfully. And, with a big sigh, he went on, 'I s'pose I'd better settle for an apple, then.'

'You might as well,' Adam agreed and for a moment, as his eyes met Julie's, she could see that he, too, was having difficulty keeping his face straight as he handed out an apple to each of the four of them.

They sat down in a sun-dappled glade to eat the apples, Shandy sitting and watching each of them in turn.

'He's waiting for the cores,' Catherine explained. 'I

tell him dogs don't like apples, but he doesn't mind—
he still wants them.'

'Oh, but our old Glen likes apple cores too,' Julie
told her. 'Holly doesn't, though.'

Catherine thought about that, her brown head tilted
to one side in a way that was heart-catchingly like her
father's, Julie realised.

'Maybe it's just boy dogs who like apples,' she said.

'Oh, no,' David returned. 'I'm a boy, and I don't like
apples.'

'Yes, but you're not a dog,' Catherine pointed out.

Apples in hand and Shandy at their heels, they wan-
dered back to the path, still arguing.

'They're just at this arguing stage,' Adam said, shaking his head. 'Whatever one of them says, the other has
to disagree. And yet at other times they're the best of
friends.'

'I haven't much experience of children,' Julie said,
smiling as she watched Shandy offer a big golden paw
in exchange for an apple core, 'but I can remember my
parents saying to each other, in an encouraging sort of
way, "It's just a phase; they'll grow out of it."'

But you don't have anyone to share this with; anyone
to tell you they'll grow out of it, she thought, seeing
the momentary shadow on Adam's lean brown face.

'Anyway,' she said, 'trying though it may be for you,
they can be so funny sometimes that it's difficult not
to laugh.'

'I know,' Adam agreed. 'The other day I thought I'd
help them to appreciate the wonders of technology and
I said, "Do you know, when I was a little boy we had
no TV?" David looked at me in amazement and then
he said, very reasonably, "But what did you watch your
videos on, Daddy?"'

They finished their apples, gave the cores to Shandy
and walked on, sometimes meeting other walkers—

many of them with dogs and children too.

I suppose we look like a family, Julie thought, and she wasn't sure, yet, how she felt about people thinking that. But, at the same time, she had a strange feeling that she was growing accustomed to the idea; that all the time she was becoming more and more fond of Adam's children and more and more comfortable with their increasing presence in her life.

'It's been a lovely morning,' she said to Adam when they got back to the car. 'I've enjoyed it so much.'

'You mean that, Julie?' Adam asked. Without waiting for an answer, he said, 'You wouldn't say it unless you did, I know that. Yes, I've enjoyed it too. But I was thinking. I can get Beauty to babysit, so how about you and I going out on Friday night? We could go to the Waterfront—have something to eat, walk around and listen to some music.' He smiled. 'Sticking with the go-slow business, of course.'

'Of course,' Julie agreed, and she smiled too. 'I'd like to do that, Adam.'

'I'll let you know before that what time I'll pick you up,' Adam said.

When the phone rang in her flat on Wednesday evening Julie thought that it would be Adam as neither of them, she knew, would be too comfortable with making private arrangements at work. She picked up the phone, smiling.

'Julie?' It wasn't Adam.

It was months since she had heard him, but he sounded just the same. There was laughter in his deep voice, and there would be laughter in his blue eyes.

'Come on, Julie, it's Mark. Mark Elliott. Remember me?'

Remember Mark Elliott? There had been a time when she'd thought that she would never be able to forget him. Julie took a deep and steadying breath.

'Of course I do, Mark,' she said, and it wasn't difficult to say his name lightly, casually. 'I'm just surprised to hear from you after all this time and—in the circumstances.'

The circumstances being, as he knew very well, that he hadn't told her that he was engaged; that he had let her believe that he was in love with her; that they had a future together.

'Oh, Julie,' he said, and his voice deepened. 'Julie, love, you haven't forgiven me. I should have told you about Cheryl, but I couldn't bear to risk losing the wonderful thing that was happening to us. I kept telling myself I should just—'

Julie broke in. 'How is Cheryl?' she asked. 'I presume you're married now?'

There was a moment's silence.

'Cheryl is fine,' he said carefully. 'Actually, no, we're not married yet. We postponed the wedding for—various reasons, but it's planned for just before Easter.'

So he isn't married yet, Julie thought with a detachment and a lack of interest in these various reasons that she wouldn't have thought possible all those months ago.

She waited.

'I got your phone number from Meg,' he said at last, still carefully. 'I knew you'd gone to Cape Town, and I knew you were working in an old-age home.'

'More a geriatric hospital, Mark, if you want to be exact,' Julie said.

'Yes, and that's why I'm phoning. Apart from wanting to know how things are with you, of course,' he added hastily. 'You see, my grandmother lives in Cape Town, and she's fallen and broken her leg. She needs hospital care, but she needs more than that and, from what I've heard, this Halvey House seems the ideal place. It would be a fairly short stay—just until the plaster is off her leg. She has a housekeeper. So—'

So?

Once again Julie waited.

'So I wondered,' Mark went on, 'if you could use your influence and get her in to that place. My folks are visiting my sister in America, you see, and that's why I've been landed—why I have to arrange something. I'm very fond of her, Julie, and I'd like to think of her in your care.'

Oh Mark, Julie thought and she couldn't help smiling, you haven't changed a bit. Switch on the charm so that other people will make your life easier.

'I haven't got that kind of influence, Mark,' she said truthfully. 'I'm a senior sister. I have nothing to do with admissions.'

'But couldn't you ask someone?' Mark said.

'There's a committee,' she told him. 'All the admissions have to go through them. Matron—Dr Brent—Miss Harrison, the social worker. I'm not even sure who the others are.'

'But wouldn't a word from you make a difference?' he asked.

'I don't think so, Mark,' Julie said. 'I don't even know if there are any beds available.'

There was one on her own floor, she knew, but what she didn't know was if there was anyone on the waiting-list. She told Mark that and then, reluctantly, she said that she would give Miss Harrison—the social worker—his grandmother's name, some details and his telephone number in Durban.

And then, when he would have gone on talking, she said, very firmly and completely untruthfully, that she was about to go out.

'Goodbye, Mark,' she said.

'Goodnight, Julie. Sweet Julie. And—thank you.'

The deep voice, and the warmth in the blue, blue

eyes. Bedroom voice, bedroom eyes, she had once said to Meg.

She put the phone down and she thought, I am glad he phoned, glad I've had this contact with him. Because I know for certain that he means nothing to me. And, whatever there was between us, it was nothing to the way I feel about Adam.

The next day she did as she had promised and spoke to Miss Harrison, who seemed very doubtful of a place being available.

'But what I can do,' she suggested, 'is phone Mr Elliott and give him some other possible places.' That done, Julie could dismiss Mark from her thoughts and look forward to spending Friday evening with Adam, just the two of them.

Taking things slowly, she reminded herself, and at the thought she found her lips curving into a smile. Adam had said it, she had agreed and then he had kissed her, and—

Or perhaps, Julie thought, her cheeks warm, perhaps I kissed him.

Friday morning was always busy, and there was a mix-up in the times arranged for the speech therapist to come and see Mrs Johnson and the physiotherapist on her daily visit. Julie managed to switch the physiotherapist to Miss Clifford first, instead of last, and by that time the speech therapist had finished.

Ted Ramsay was going home for the weekend, and the hospital Kombi was ready for him half an hour earlier than the arranged time. Julie and Prudence hurried to get him ready, to phone his wife and tell her that he was on his way and to get him and his wheelchair downstairs, ready to go.

The junior nurse-aide had made coffee for them when they got back, and the next job, Julie knew, would be to complete the baths and the bed-baths. She had just finished her coffee, when the phone rang.

'Sister Maynard? Dr Brent here. Could you possibly come down to my office?'

Adam had a small office on the ground floor but she had only been in it once or twice, and it was most unusual for him to send for her. Julie gave her staff swift instructions, and then ran down the two floors to Adam's office. His door was closed, and she knocked.

'Come in,' Adam said.

There was a man with him, but Julie barely glanced at him as she said, formally and correctly, 'You wanted to see me, Dr Brent?' Adam looked up from the folder on his desk.

'Yes, Sister. We're admitting a new patient right away. Mrs Elliott. I believe you know her grandson.'

Mark Elliott stood up and came towards her, taking both her hands in his.

'Julie, it's so good to see you again. And as lovely as ever.'

Julie tried to free her hands, but he wouldn't let her go. He looked down at her, his eyes very blue in the brown of his face.

'Thank you for what you did,' Mark said softly. 'I'm so grateful. It's been such a worry with me in Durban and Gran here, helpless.'

At last Julie managed to draw her hands away from his.

'So Miss Harrison was able to help you?' she said, surprised after what the social worker had said.

Mark shrugged, the elegant, easy shrug she remembered when he chose not to reply directly.

'I'm delighted to think of Gran here, and you looking after her, Julie. It's going to make the world of difference to her. And to me,' Mark said. He turned to Adam. 'Thanks so much for your help, Dr Brent. I'll see that her GP gets the complete file to you, and it's just after two that the ambulance is booked for, right? Then I'd better get back and get her ready. See you later, Julie.'

When he had gone Julie looked at Adam, his brown head bent over the folder. 'I take it Mrs Elliott is to be on my floor, Dr Brent?' she said hesitantly. Adam looked up.

'Oh, yes,' he said, his voice expressionless. 'Mr Elliott was adamant about that.'

He was angry. Very angry.

'How could he insist on her being on my floor?' Julie said. 'He's lucky to have got her in. Miss Harrison said—'

Adam put his pen down.

'I gather that Mr Elliott asked who else was on the board, discovered that either he or his grandmother knew at least two members, got in touch with them and that was that. Your—friend seems to have a fair bit of influence.'

It was Mark he was angry with, Julie told herself, not her. She had done nothing.

'I've left a message for Matron—she was at a meeting,' Adam said, lifting his pen again. 'No doubt you'll want to make suitable arrangements for your new patient, Sister.'

It was very clear, she realised with dismay, that this was a dismissal. And pretty clear, too, that at least some of his anger was directed towards her. Julie hesitated, wanting to say something but uncertain as to what. In the end she said, steadily, professionally, 'Certainly, Dr Brent.'

He'll have cooled down by tonight, she told herself as she and Prudence checked the small private room that Mark's grandmother would be in. I'll be able to explain. She wasn't sure just what she should be explaining, but something seemed to be called for.

There was very little time, during the rest of the day,
for her to think any more about Adam's reaction. Matron
came up half an hour later, bringing Mrs Elliott's folder
with her.

'Fracture of the femur in the distal third,' she said.
'It's an uncomplicated fracture so she's had a com-
pression plate put in. The leg was in traction while she
was in hospital. It should still be immobilised for about
six weeks, but the orthopaedic surgeon says she doesn't
need any more traction.' She hesitated. 'I gather you
know her grandson, Sister?'

'I *did* know him, yes,' Julie replied, annoyed at herself
for sounding—she knew—awkward, perhaps even
defensive. 'I haven't seen him for months, and I never
did know him really well.' And that is certainly true,
she thought. I thought I did, for that short time.

Matron's grey eyes were thoughtful, perhaps even
questioning, but after a moment she nodded and went
on to discuss Mrs Elliott's medication.

The ambulance arrived about the same time as Mark
did. Julie happened to see, from the window of the duty
room, Mark's tall figure striding from a sleek German
sports car across to the ambulance. Soon after that the
lift arrived, and her new patient was carried out into the
corridor.

'Along here—Room Six,' Julie told the ambulance-
men. 'Hello, Mrs Elliott, we'll have you settled in
no time.'

Mrs Elliott, even lying on a stretcher, was a dignified
and very correct lady. Her silvery hair was perfectly
done, and her lipstick was the same shade as her cotton
dressing-gown. But, in spite of that, her blue eyes—so
like Mark's—were just a little apprehensive, Julie
thought when she and Mark were alone with his grandmother. Apprehensive, and she could see now that there

were lines of strain and weariness about the old lady's mouth.

Julie raised the back of the bed and put another pillow behind Mrs Elliott's shoulder. Then, gently and expertly, she arranged a pillow to support the leg that was in plaster.

'Thank you, Sister,' Mrs Elliott murmured, and she smiled. Mark's smile, Julie thought, but I'm not going to hold that against her. 'That feels much more comfortable.'

'Would you like a cup of tea, Mrs Elliott?' Julie asked. For the first time she looked directly at Mark. 'Perhaps your grandson would like some tea, too, before he goes?'

Mark bent and kissed his grandmother's cheek.

'Didn't I tell you she was wonderful?' he said to her. 'Julie will look after you, Gran. I'll feel so much better about you.'

For a moment there was something in the old lady's eyes that made Julie think that perhaps she was fairly clear-sighted about her good-looking and charming grandson.

'I'm sure you will, dear,' she said. 'And this is Sister Maynard to me, even if she is an old friend of yours.'

An old friend? Mark's eyes, meeting Julie's, glanced away quickly.

'I'll send Nurse Solomon along with tea, Mrs Elliott,' Julie said. 'I'm sure Dr Brent will be in to see you some time this afternoon.'

She went back to her office and the charts she had left when her new patient arrived. Half an hour later Mark put his head round the door.

'Thought I'd just say goodbye, Julie,' he said cheerfully. 'I'm off back to Durban tomorrow—some people I have to see about a deal we're in the middle of—but

I'll be flying down next week so I'll be here to see
Gran. And you.'

Julie ignored that, and couldn't resist a downward
glance at Ted Ramsay's chart on the desk in front of her.

'I know, you're busy,' Mark said. 'I just wondered,
couldn't we have dinner together tonight—for old
times' sake?'

For old times' sake? How could he have the nerve to
say that to her? Julie wasn't sure whether she felt angry
or amused but this wasn't the time or the place to be
either, so she merely said, quietly, that she wasn't free
that evening.

'Maybe next time,' Mark said, and before she could
make it very clear that her answer would be the same
he said goodbye and walked along to the lift.

Five minutes later she looked up and saw Adam,
hurrying along the corridor past her door. She stood up
quickly, and caught up with him as he knocked on the
door of Mrs Elliott's room.

'Ah, Sister Maynard, I didn't want to disturb you.
Thought I'd look in on Mrs Elliott,' Adam said, looking
a little discomfited as he seldom visited any of her
patients without at least telling her that he was going
to. He held out his hand. 'Mrs Elliott, I'm Dr Brent. I just
met your grandson downstairs—he says you're nicely
settled in already.'

'Yes, I am, Dr Brent,' Mrs Elliot said. 'I can see that
Sister Maynard and Nurse Solomon and the rest of the
staff are going to look after me very well indeed. Wasn't
it lucky for me that Mark thought of Halvey House
because of Sister Maynard being here?'

No one else, Julie thought, would have noticed the
brief hesitation before Adam replied. 'Yes, it was,' he
agreed.

He asked a few questions about the accident she had
had, and told her that he had been in touch with the

orthopaedic surgeon who had operated on her leg.

'It's just a matter of time now, as I'm sure Dr Field told you,' he said. 'Sister Maynard and her staff will look after you, and in a little while we'll consider physiotherapy to get you mobile again.'

The silvery head nodded.

'Good,' the old lady said briskly. 'I may be seventy, but I do lead a very active life, Dr Brent. I play bridge twice a week and Scrabble twice a week. I meet friends to walk in the gardens at Kirstenbosch and I go to the theatre. And I'm not prepared to let a broken leg do more than put a temporary stop to any of that!'

Adam smiled and Julie thought, with relief, that whatever animosity he might feel towards Mark he wasn't going to let it affect his attitude to Mrs Elliott.

'Good for you, Mrs Elliott,' he said. He patted her hand. 'We'll have you back on that bridge circuit in no time. And you might find you can raise a good game of Scrabble right here. Sister Maynard might be able to organise some of our Scrabble players to come to your room, at least until we can get you into a wheelchair and moving around.'

He looked at Julie. 'I'd like to have a look at Mrs Elliott's chart, Sister,' he said. 'I just want to check on her medication.'

Back in the duty room he looked at the chart, and after a few moments nodded. 'Yes, that should do,' he murmured. He looked at his watch. 'I'll look in on Miss Clifford, Sister. Don't worry, I can see you have plenty to do. I'll just go along.' At the door he turned.

'Sister Maynard,' he said abruptly, 'perhaps, in the circumstances, we should leave that arrangement for tonight.'

Julie knew that her bewilderment must have shown on her face. 'Leave it?' she repeated. 'But—'

'I thought you would prefer to take the chance to see

Mr Elliott.' Julie could feel warm, defensive colour flood her face.

'No, I—I told him I wasn't free,' she said quickly.

She could see the controlled anger on Adam's face, and dismay filled her at the thought of missing out on the evening she had looked forward to so much—this time alone with Adam.

'And, even if I had been, I wouldn't have wanted to see him.' She smiled tentatively, in spite of the lack of any answering smile from Adam. 'I'm looking forward so much to this evening.'

His brows were drawn together and, for a moment, she thought he was going to say something more. Then he shrugged.

'As you like,' he said coolly.

As I like? Julie thought, bewildered. Surely he hadn't actually wanted to break their date? What I should have said, Julie thought as he nodded and went out, was the plain truth. I want to see you, Adam, I want to be with you. I haven't the slightest wish to see Mark Elliott, or to spend any time at all with him. But perhaps that would have been overreacting.

As she dressed that evening—hesitating between a sea-green dress, long and sleek, and the sunshine-yellow one with the shoestring straps that Adam had said once, a little diffidently, that he liked—she told herself that, after all, it was only reasonable for him to suggest that perhaps she might like to see an 'old friend'.

There was probably nothing more in it than that, and as for his earlier anger—well, she knew, didn't she, that he didn't like people using influence to jump the waiting-list for Halvey House?

She put on the yellow dress and left her hair loose, smiling as she remembered Catherine saying that her hair was like a fairy princess's. Tonight, she thought, there would be just the two of us, Adam and me. Next time there would be Catherine and David too. And Shandy.

She had said she would go up to the cottage, rather than have Adam pick her up outside the big house. Without either of them needing to say anything, it was easier to avoid interested glances.

As it was, the only interested glances were from Catherine and David, Catherine touching the silky folds of her dress wonderingly and David asking if they would be having chips to eat.

'I don't know,' Julie told him, laughing. 'There are other things to eat besides chips, you know, David.'

'Yes, but chips are the best,' the little boy said earnestly.

Adam was quiet in the car as he drove down from the slopes of the mountain towards the sea. But the Friday night traffic was heavy and he had to concentrate, Julie reminded herself.

It was a warm and still evening, and the Waterfront was busy. The smell of the sea and the sight of the ships in Table Bay gave a real holiday feeling, Julie said.

Yes, it did, Adam agreed politely.

'We're lucky it's such a perfect evening, and no south-easter blowing,' Julie went on.

'Yes, we are,' Adam replied.

They were standing beside the landing-place for the old Penny Ferry, with the sea ahead of them and the mountain behind. A perfect evening, a wonderful place, and we are standing here talking about the weather, Julie thought.

She looked at Adam's face, remote—like a stranger's. But he isn't a stranger, she reminded herself. He is the man I—care for a great deal.

'Adam,' she said, gently, 'what's wrong?'

He turned to her.

'You know very well what's wrong,' he said, and the leashed anger in his voice dismayed her. 'I don't like what you and your friend Mark Elliott have done to get his grandmother in ahead of people who have been on the waiting-list for some time. I don't like it at all.'

'I didn't do anything,' Julie returned spiritedly. 'I told Mark I had no influence as far as admissions were concerned, and I said I'd give Miss Harrison his phone number. That's all. That is all, Adam. You said yourself that Mark had found out the names of the board members, and used a connection with a couple of them. I had nothing to do with that.'

There was no warmth in Adam's grey eyes as he looked down at her.

'I wouldn't quite agree,' he said. 'I gather he told Colonel Fitzpatrick and Mrs Dalton that it's because of you that he wants his grandmother here. Mrs Dalton, in particular, was very touched that a rising young businessman like Mark Elliott should have such concern over who was to look after his grandmother.'

'Because of me?' Julie repeated, taken aback. And then, recovering, 'Oh, Adam, that's just Mark's way of getting what he wants. It doesn't mean anything.'

'Doesn't it?' Adam asked. 'I'm not so sure about that, Julie.' The line of his jaw was bleak.

'You told me, once, that there was no one special,' he said very quietly. 'Why didn't you tell me about Mark Elliott?'

CHAPTER EIGHT

'BUT I did tell you about Mark,' Julie said, bewildered. 'That day on the beach I told you about him. The patient who didn't bother to tell me he was engaged—remember? His fiancée was away on a skiing holiday when he came in to have his appendix out.'

'Yes, you did tell me that much,' Adam agreed, his voice level. 'But you didn't tell me how important he was in your life.'

It was a moment before Julie could reply.

'Yes, he was important to me at the time,' she said quietly. 'I was very hurt when I found out that he hadn't told me he was engaged. But that was months ago. I haven't given him a thought for ages. Not since I came to Halvey House. By the time I told you about him he didn't matter at all to me.' All at once she couldn't keep her voice steady. 'You should know that, Adam.' He was silent, his face turned away from her.

'I don't believe this,' Julie said shakily. 'Adam, Mark is engaged. He's getting married very soon. He means nothing to me—nothing—and he just used me to get his grandmother into Halvey House.'

Now he did look at her.

'I got the clear impression,' he said, 'that one of the reasons he was so glad to get his grandmother in was so that you and he could renew your—friendship.'

It was now Julie who turned away, unable to take what had become cool hostility in his eyes.

'I don't know how you got that impression,' she said, fighting to keep her voice controlled, 'because it isn't true.'

Without a word he began to walk away, his hands in his pockets. She caught up with him.

'Who do you believe, Adam?' she asked him. 'Me, or a man you've just met? A man who will use people, and use the truth, in whatever way will suit him best?'

It was a long time before he replied.

'I don't know, Julie,' he said tiredly at last. 'I just don't know. I wish I didn't have to say that, but that's how I feel.'

There was a knot of misery in Julie's throat, and she could feel the sting of tears she would not allow herself to shed.

'In that case,' she said, very quietly, 'I don't think there's much point in going on with the evening. I'd like to go home, Adam.'

Home.

Suddenly, achingly, she knew that she didn't mean her little bedsitter at the top of Halvey House. She meant the rambling old house to the north of Durban, with her mother and her father, her brothers, the old dog and the young one. Everything that was dear and familiar; everything that seemed so very far away.

Neither of them said anything on the way back. There was nothing to say, Julie thought, nothing at all.

He stopped the car outside Halvey House, and she got out.

'Goodnight, Adam,' she said quietly.

'Julie, I—'

For a moment the unhappiness on his face made her want to reach out to him—to put her arms around him. She thought later that if only he had said something— if only he had held out his hand to her then it would have been all right.

But he did neither, and after a moment she walked away from him—up the wide steps and into the house, closing the door behind her.

She walked the three flights up to her room slowly, feeling as if she was very old and very tired. But she didn't cry—even when she was in the small and secure haven of her room, sitting on the padded window-seat. She was beyond tears, beyond anything but an aching numbness. The small spurt of anger that had made her ask him who he believed had gone.

This hurt, somehow, was much deeper than the hurt she had felt when she'd found out that Mark had deceived her. She had come to care so much for Adam, so much more than she had cared for anyone before.

Adam, and his children.

She stood up and walked over to the long mirror on the wall. Just before she'd gone out this evening she had stood there and had pirouetted, her silky yellow skirt billowing around her bare tanned legs and her hair loose on her shoulders. That Julie seemed like a different person, for the girl looking out at her now had no sparkle about her, no life. Her brown eyes were shadowed, and her face drained of colour.

'Nonsense!' Julie said aloud, and the girl in the mirror lifted her chin.

'Are you a man or a mouse?' she asked herself severely, and the foolish words brought a watery smile to the girl in the mirror.

I can't change what's happened, she thought, but I can change this—this drippiness. All right, Adam should not have reacted the way he did, but there are good enough reasons for him to have difficulty handling what he sees as a lack of trust.

She should, she thought, have followed that instinct to reach out to him. What had stopped her? she wondered. Foolish pride, fear of rejection—oh, there were good enough reasons, but she knew now that that momentary instinct had been right.

And what now?

She made herself a mug of coffee and sat on the window-seat, drinking it, as she thought about the situation. And knowing, almost right away, that she would have to make the first move. But not immediately. She would leave things over the weekend and find a chance—make a chance—early next week to speak to him. She wasn't sure what she would say, but one thing she was completely certain of. What there was between them was much too important to lose.

With that decision made, she went to bed and slept more soundly than she would have thought possible, waking to the realisation that here she was with her weekend off—a weekend she had thought she would be spending at least part of with Adam and the children.

When Ryan's cousin from Camps Bay phoned to ask her to join them for a braai she accepted immediately. The young accountant she had gone out with was there, and she enjoyed meeting him again. There was talk, there was laughter and there was easy and undemanding company. She enjoyed the day thoroughly but at the end of it she knew, even more clearly, how much she had missed being with Adam and the children—knew with even more certainty that she had to put things right between Adam and her.

She swam in the pool in the garden twice on Sunday, half expecting to see Adam and the children and thinking that perhaps even now she could make that move. But no one came down the path from the cottage.

The next morning, as Matron was leaving after her round, she stopped at the door.

'Oh, Sister Maynard, it will be old Dr Bates coming around later today,' she said. 'I don't think you've met him—he was in charge before Dr Brent came. He's filling in for a couple of days.'

Julie's heart turned over. 'Is Dr Brent ill?' she asked carefully.

Matron looked surprised. 'Oh, no, Sister, he's gone off to a conference on geriatric medicine in Grahamstown. I think he suddenly decided that he would go. I know he had to arrange for the children to stay with schoolfriends. Of course, you were off at the weekend—he probably told Sister Morkel before he left on Saturday morning, and she forgot to pass it on.'

So talking to Adam will have to wait, Julie thought, and she wasn't sure whether she felt disappointed or relieved.

He had mentioned the conference, she remembered now, and he had said that he would talk to Matron about Julie going to the next one. But he hadn't, at that time, had any thought of going himself. It had been a sudden decision, and she had no doubts about his reasons for wanting to get away from the cottage and Halvey House. And, above all, from me, she told herself.

But that didn't change her own decision to take the first step in bridging this awful chasm between them. She would just have to wait, and perhaps it wasn't a bad thing for them not to see each other at all for these few days.

On a purely professional level, she knew that he would be pleased at the improvement in Mrs Johnson. Since Julie had talked to her daughters and asked them to accept their mother's wish to face up to the possibility of her death she could see a real change in her patient. Somehow, now that this was out in the open between them, Mrs Johnson had undoubtedly become less anxious, less stressed.

'The cardiologist was very pleased with her,' Julie told Matron. 'He's even thinking about reducing her betablock medication.'

Matron nodded.

'You did the right thing to step in, Sister,' she said.

'I was afraid I was doing more than that,' Julie admitted. 'It came close to interfering.'

'Not at all, Sister,' Matron said briskly. 'The welfare of your patients must always be your first consideration, and that is what made you speak out. Now, how is Mrs Elliott settling down?'

Quite well, Julie told her. She hesitated and then said, cautiously, that Mrs Elliott was quite a demanding patient.

'In a very nice way, of course,' she added quickly. Matron smiled.

'I can imagine that, from the little I've seen of her,' she agreed. 'Don't let her try to take advantage of the fact that you and her grandson know each other.'

'I don't think she would do that,' Julie said.

She had wondered, herself, if this might be a problem, but she could see already that although Mark had been all too ready to use any influence he could his grandmother wouldn't do the same.

'Thank you, Sister Maynard, that feels much more comfortable,' Mrs Elliott said gratefully when Julie had adjusted the cushion supporting her plaster. 'I'm perfectly happy. I'm sure you have people who need your attention much more than I do.'

'We're quiet this afternoon,' Julie told her. 'We've got most of the patients downstairs on the big stoep for tea, and any visitors are down there too. Except Mrs Johnson—her daughters will only be here later.'

'I didn't want any visitors today,' Mrs Elliott said. 'I told my friends they can come tomorrow afternoon after I've had my hair done.' For the first time she looked a little anxious. 'This girl who comes here, is she quite good? I haven't let anyone but Raymond touch my hair for years, you know.'

'Your hair is lovely,' Julie said truthfully. 'And I can see how beautifully cut it is. Marian is good. She won't be as good as your Raymond, I'm sure, but she'll wash your hair, and set it on rollers or blow-dry it—whichever you want—and she's accustomed to working with patients who are in bed.'

The old lady patted her silvery hair. 'I'm glad I'll have my hair done before Mark comes back.'

'When is he coming?' Julie asked.

'I think he said Thursday or Friday,' Mark's grandmother said. 'He has some deal he has to finish off in Durban, then he has to be here for a meeting.' She looked up at Julie. 'Do you know Cheryl, Sister Maynard?'

Julie shook her head. 'I haven't met her,' she said, and she hoped that she hadn't sounded too abrupt. 'I only knew Mark for a short time, Mrs Elliott. He came in to have his appendix out when I was on Surgical at the Royal.' Then, very carefully, she said that she thought his fiancée had been on a skiing holiday at the time.

'Yes, I do remember that,' Mrs Elliott said, and added, 'I should be all right to travel to Durban for the wedding, Dr Norton says. I wouldn't like to miss that. They'll make a handsome couple.'

'I'm sure they will,' Julie agreed.

For a moment there was a twinkle which was almost mischievous in the old lady's eyes.

'And she's tough enough to keep Mark in order,' she said. 'Oh, yes, I'm pretty sure she knows that will be necessary. I know my grandson, Sister. He can be too charming for his own good.'

I know that very well, Julie thought, and she wondered how much Mrs Elliott knew of her 'friendship' with Mark.

The old doctor who was standing in for Adam was

exactly how Julie had imagined Adam himself would
be—pleasant, fatherly, a little slow, and always with
time to spare to talk to each patient. But perhaps, she
thought, he was a little out of touch, and she was glad
that there were no emergencies while Adam was away.

He came back on Wednesday morning, and Julie was
glad that Dr Bates had mentioned this the day before so
that she wasn't unprepared when he came into her office.

'Good morning, Sister,' he said formally. 'Morning,
Nurse Solomon. Everything in order here?'

Julie stood up. 'Everything is fine, Dr Brent,' she
replied, just as formally. 'Did you find the conference
interesting?'

'Yes, I did,' Adam replied. 'Well worthwhile
going to it.'

She went round the patients with him, correctly, professionally, knowing very well that this certainly was
not the time or the place for her to be able to say anything
private to him. But wondering, too, when it would be
possible.

The next morning he was later coming to do his
rounds, because he was at the Clinic until after eleven.

'I can still smell the theatre on you, Dr Brent,' Miss
Clifford said, wrinkling her nose.

'And not your kind of theatre, either,' Adam returned,
and he smiled. Gently he took her swollen hands in his.

'Is that new cortisone cream helping, Miss Clifford?'
he asked.

'I think it is, Dr Brent,' Miss Clifford said. She looked
at Julie, and smiled. 'But I sometimes think it's the way
our Sister Sunshine rubs it into my hands—so gently,
but so thoroughly—that's the real help.'

For a moment Adam's eyes met Julie's, and her heart
turned over. Although he was still professional, still
detached, some small degree of warmth was in his eyes.

'Yes, Miss Clifford,' he said quietly, 'Sister Maynard will certainly look after you.'

Perhaps, she thought that night in her room, while he was away he has been doing some thinking too. Perhaps, when I speak to him, when I make that move, he'll meet me—if not halfway, at least part of the way.

She was still very certain that that first move would have to come from her. And she was also very certain that she had to make that move, regardless of her own pride—regardless of her very real fear of rejection from Adam. Perhaps, she thought, tomorrow night I'll walk up to the cottage after the children are asleep.

The next day there was a message from Matron to say that Dr Brent would only be there in the afternoon, as he had had to go to the Clinic unexpectedly.

'Dr Brent will be along later this afternoon,' Julie told Captain O'Connor when he rang his bell to ask her where the doctor was. 'Did you want to see him particularly?'

The captain's leg had healed nicely but there was still the danger of rejection, and both Adam and Julie kept a constant check on it.

The old Irishman shook his head.

'No, I just enjoy seeing him,' he said. 'One of the high spots of me day, mavourneen, and of course you're the other.'

'I suppose your life is less exciting now that Mrs Smit has gone, and you don't have the fun of playing Miss Clifford and her off against each other,' Julie said, smiling.

'Yes, it was a bit of fun,' the captain agreed, unrepentant. 'But Miss Clifford and I have settled back into our usual routine, and who knows what the future will bring in the way of interesting ladies?' He shook his head. 'That Mrs Elliott now, I won't be getting anywhere with her. We've had the odd game of Scrabble, but I can see that's my dead limit.' His faded blue eyes were suddenly bright. 'Makes me feel a bit like Lady Chatterley's Lover—or would-be, anyway.'

Unable to stop herself, Julie burst out laughing at the thought of Mrs Elliott as Lady Chatterley, and Captain O'Connor as the game-keeper.

'A bit steamy for Halvey House, I think,' she said at last, and the old man agreed that it might be.

Still smiling, Julie went back to her office. He is an old rogue, she thought, but I'm very fond of him.

There were charts to be filled in, and it was the day for checking the drug cupboard. She got out her list to check off the supplies, and had just started when there was a knock at the door.

'Come in,' she said, not looking up as she kept her pen on the check-list for Mrs Johnson's betablock medication.

'Julie.'

Mark Elliott stood in the doorway, a huge bunch of red roses in his arms.

'Isn't there a vase in your grandmother's room?' Julie asked, standing up. 'I'll get Prudence to check and we can find one, if not.'

Mark shook his head. 'These aren't for Gran,' he said. 'They're for you.'

She thought, later, that her dismay must have been all too obvious.

'Oh, Mark, you shouldn't,' she said, disconcerted. He put the beautiful roses in her arms.

'No ulterior motive, Julie,' he said, and there was no guile in his blue eyes. 'I've been hearing from Gran how well you look after her, and I appreciate that, Julie. She's an independent old lady, and you've made this much easier for her than I expected it to be. I'm grateful for that.'

He smiled, and although the familiar charm was there

there was something more. He really means it, Julie thought, taken aback.

'Believe it or not,' he said, 'I'm very fond of her, and I do worry about her. Or I did, until I saw her today. So I went down to that flower shop on the corner to get you these.'

'Oh, Mark,' Julie said a little unsteadily. She had had grateful relatives of patients before but somehow this, coming from Mark Elliott, touched her more than she would have thought possible.

'Tears, Julie?' Mark said, and there was a tenderness in his voice she had never known in him.

'Just because I'm very touched,' Julie told him, feeling that her immediate reaction of dismay had been unnecessary. 'Thank you.'

He took out his handkerchief, and very gently wiped her eyes. 'You are a very sweet girl, Julie,' he said softly.

Briefly, his lips brushed hers. But not briefly enough.

'I'm sorry to interrupt, Sister Maynard,' Adam said from the open doorway.

And any hint of thaw she had seen in his eyes the day before had gone completely as he stood there, looking at her, with her arms full of red roses and with Mark Elliott's kiss still warm on her lips.

'Dr Brent,' Julie said, dismayed. 'I thought you were at the Clinic this morning.'

'I finished early—one operation was postponed,' Adam replied brusquely. And then, with ice in his voice, he said, 'If you could spare the time, Sister Maynard, I'd like to do my round now.'

'Certainly, Dr Brent,' Julie replied. There was nothing she could say about what he had just seen, she knew that. Nothing that he would accept and understand.

Mark Elliott, glancing from her to the doctor, would have had to be blind not to see that something was far from right, she thought afterwards.

'I hope I'm not out of line, Dr Brent,' he said smoothly, 'but I did want to thank Julie—sorry, Sister Maynard—for looking after my grandmother so well. I'm very grateful.'

'I can see that,' Adam Brent replied, and the ice was still there. 'Sister Maynard can always be relied on to do her job competently, Mr Elliott.' But she can't be relied on for anything else, were the words left unsaid.

'If you'll excuse us, Mr Elliott,' Adam said.

As she followed him from the room Julie had to call on all her professional training to put these few disastrous moments behind her—to focus only on the responsibility of accompanying Adam on his round. He, of course, was as professional as she was, and they discussed Miss Clifford's new medication, the physiotherapy Captain O'Connor was having, Ted Ramsay's adverse reaction to a change in his muscle-relaxant pills, the best timing for Mrs Elliott to start gentle physiotherapy and Mrs Johnson's next visit from the cardiologist.

Julie made notes of anything Adam wanted done, as she always did, and somehow she managed to reply to Adam's questions, in spite of the tight knot of misery in her throat.

'Has Dr Brent gone?' Prudence asked, surprised, when Julie went back into the duty room alone. 'I made coffee for him. Come to think of it, though, he seems to have been in too much of a hurry the past few days.'

Yes, since Mark decided to come back into my life, Julie thought, because it suited him to—because he needed to use me to get his grandmother into Halvey House. She was angry with him about that, but yet he'd meant it when he'd said that he was grateful to her for what she had done for his grandmother. And she had been touched by that. Touched, but nothing more.

I know that. I should think that Mark knows that, but

Adam just wouldn't believe it, she told herself unhappily. He must be all too certain now that his initial judgement of me was all too right.

A girl like you, he had once said, she remembered bleakly. A girl who had told him that Mark Elliott meant nothing to her now—but a girl he had found being kissed by that same Mark Elliott.

And to be fair, she thought with reluctance, what he had seen could undoubtedly have made him think she was anything but indifferent to Mark. She hadn't been pushing him away, or resisting in any way. It hadn't been a kiss that needed that sort of reaction. But Adam couldn't know that.

When you came down to it, it had just been one brief kiss but one too many. And one that she was pretty certain she wouldn't have any chance to explain to Adam.

That afternoon, when the bell rang for the end of visiting time, Mark put his head round the door of the office, where Julie was working.

'That was a bit of bad timing, I'm afraid,' he said. 'Sorry about that. Dr Brent obviously doesn't like his nurses collaborating with the relatives.'

'It isn't very professional,' Julie told him truthfully. Mark shrugged.

'He was a bit over the top, though,' he said. 'Some doctors would have taken it in their stride.'

Some, yes, Julie thought. But not Adam. Certainly not where I'm concerned.

'It doesn't matter,' she said, and even to herself she sounded unconvincing. Mark was looking at her thoughtfully, and she knew that the last thing she wanted was for him to begin wondering if there was anything more than a professional relationship between Adam and her. With some difficulty, she smiled. 'Thank you for the roses, anyway,' she said quickly. 'They look lovely in my room.'

Neither she nor Adam had ever discussed the need to keep their growing friendship a secret from the staff at Halvey House, or at least something that they didn't want to make too obvious. It had just happened naturally. And no one did seem to have realised. But there was no way, Julie realised with a heavy heart, that the way things had changed between them could go unnoticed, either by the staff or by at least some of the patients.

'What's with Dr Brent?' Prudence asked one day. 'He barely gives you the time of day, and he used to sit down and have a cup of coffee and talk about the patients. I've even heard him call you Sister Sunshine to Captain O'Connor.'

Julie hesitated, but some explanation did seem necessary.

'Mark Elliott and I used to know each other,' she said carefully. 'I think Dr Brent feels that I—that I may not be as professionally detached as I should be with him.' Prudence's eyebrows rose.

'And are you?' she asked eagerly. 'Detached, I mean. I wouldn't find it too easy to be detached from a gorgeous man like that.'

'I'm detached,' Julie said briefly.

But a few days later, when Mark was in Cape Town again and came to visit his grandmother, she found Prudence looking thoughtfully first at Mark and then at her.

In a way, the younger girl's questioning about Mark was easier to handle than anything to do with Adam.

'Dr Brent looks very sad,' little Miss Clifford said unexpectedly one day. 'He used to look like that after his wife died and I'd been thinking, over the past weeks, how much younger and more carefree and—happier he was looking.' She shook her head. 'Now he's just the way he was before.'

Captain O'Connor had noticed too.

'Doesn't seem like himself, Dr Brent,' he said. 'Oh, you can't fault him in the way he looks after us, but he's become withdrawn, remote, again. Don't you think so, Sister?'

Julie turned away from the old man and straightened his bedcover.

'I haven't really thought about it, Captain O'Connor,' she replied, completely untruthfully. 'Now, how about that return Scrabble match with Mrs Johnson?'

Something which took her a little by surprise was to find that she actually missed the children almost as much as she missed Adam. She missed the funny things they said, the way Catherine put her head on one side—so like her father—the way David's small freckled nose wrinkled when he smiled, the feel of a small hand in each of hers as they walked on the beach or through the forest. She hadn't realised that she would feel like this, and it shook her.

One afternoon, when she took Miss Clifford down to the big verandah in her wheelchair, she found the children there with Shandy. They were talking to a small group of patients from the first floor when they saw her.

'Julie!' David called, with pleasure. Catherine nudged him.

'We have to say Sister Maynard when she's in her uniform,' she reminded him in a whisper that brought smiles to the faces of all the elderly people nearby.

The big golden dog reached her first, and she patted him and rubbed his ears as he gave little barks.

'Quiet, Shandy,' Catherine told him sternly. 'You know we have to behave very well when we come here.' She sat down on the swing seat and watched as Julie pushed Miss Clifford's chair closer to the table and poured tea for her. 'Matron asked Daddy if we would please come again,' she said.

'Cos everyone liked us so much,' David added. And then went on, 'You haven't been to see us for so long, Julie—Sister Maynard. I made a lovely Lego castle, with a dragon coming to attack it, and I wanted to let you see it.' He sighed heavily. 'But now I've had to take it down to make a train.'

'I'm sorry about that, David,' Julie said very quietly.

Catherine's grey eyes were very dark, her small face serious.

'We went to see Granny and Grandpa on Sunday, and me and David wanted you to come with us but Daddy said you were busy.'

'Granny was dispointed too,' David said.

'Disappointed,' Catherine corrected him. 'Julie—I mean Sister Maynard—it's soon going to be my birthday, and long ago I told Daddy that I don't want a party. I just want to go to the top of Table Mountain in the night, just you and Daddy and me and David. It's all floodlit, and it looks so beautiful.'

'Not Shandy,' David explained, 'cos they wouldn't let dogs go on the cable-car.'

Julie didn't know what to say.

'I would have thought you'd like having a party, Catherine,' she said a little lamely. 'Everyone in party dresses, and—and balloons and games.'

Catherine shook her head, and her long brown hair hid her face for a moment. 'I don't want a party,' she said with certainty.

'Catherine,' Adam said warningly, appearing unexpectedly behind them. The little girl coloured. 'I told you Sister Maynard is busy, and she does have other friends to see.'

Julie felt her own cheeks grow warm, and her heart went out to the child. She hated leaving Catherine thinking that other friends were so important that she had no time for them, but she couldn't think of an acceptable alternative explanation.

'I'm sorry, Catherine,' she said very quietly.

For a moment Adam's eyes met hers, then he looked away.

Julie told Miss Clifford that she would come back down for her in a little while, then she said goodbye to the children and went back to her floor with an ache in her heart.

A few days later, just as Julie was going off duty at seven, Mrs Johnson's bell rang.

'I'll see to her,' said Brenda Morkel, who was taking over for the night, but Julie shook her head.

'I'll look in on my way out,' she said.

Mrs Johnson, leaning back against her pillows, tried to smile when Julie went in.

'I'm sorry, Sister,' she said apologetically. 'The minute I rang the bell I wished I hadn't. There isn't really anything wrong, it's just—' She hesitated.

One swift but careful glance alerted that sixth sense which Julie knew she had to listen to.

'Do you have any pain, Mrs Johnson?' she asked, all too conscious of the history of angina. The old lady shook her head.

'Not pain, no,' she said. 'But this arm—not the stroke one, the other one—feels a little numb. But not painful, Sister, really. And there's—now this does sound so foolish—'

'Foolish or not, you tell me about it,' Julie said firmly.

'It's a heavy sort of feeling. I just don't feel good. Not physically, but in my mind.'

Julie knew all too well that this sort of apprehension was very characteristic of an impending attack of angina—that it would almost be sufficient for a diagnosis.

She put her hand on Mrs Johnson's forehead and, as she had expected, there was a slight dampness.

'I want you to take one of your nitroglycerin tablets, Mrs Johnson,' she said steadily. 'I'm just going to ask Dr Brent to come and have a look at you.' She rang the bell, and when Prudence appeared she asked the younger girl to send for Dr Brent.

'That's right, under your tongue,' she said as she positioned the nitroglycerin tablet. She smiled at the woman in the bed. 'Pretty efficient, these things. You should feel a little better right away.'

The success of the medication would, she knew, confirm that this was an attack of angina. And sure enough, a moment or two later Mrs Johnson said that her arm and her hand did feel better.

'And I'm beginning to feel that terrible depressing feeling lifting,' she said. She managed to smile. 'But I felt better anyway, Sister, as soon as you came in. And here's Dr Brent. I'm sure I don't need to be disturbing him.'

Quickly and professionally Julie told Adam what Mrs Johnson had told her, and what she herself had done.

Adam, with the old lady's wrist in his hand and his eyes on her face, nodded.

'Good girl,' he said, and her heart turned over for, in his absorption with their patient, his hostility had disappeared. 'It might be a good idea to take another pill, Mrs Johnson. Let's just wait a few minutes, and see how you feel.'

The clamminess had left Mrs Johnson's forehead, as well as the look of anxiety. But it was a long five minutes, Julie thought, as they both watched and waited. At last Adam nodded, satisfied.

'You don't need another one,' he said. 'I think I'd

like to have Dr Morton come and have a look at you—
I'll ring him now. Meanwhile, have a little sleep if you
feel like it.'

'What I do feel like,' Mrs Johnson said with revived
spirit, 'is a cup of tea.'

'I'll get Sister Morkel to arrange that,' Julie promised.
She and Adam walked along the corridor together.

'She'll do,' Adam said, 'thanks to your quick action.
I'm glad we didn't have to give her a second one,
though. I don't like the side-effects—the headaches, the
dizziness—especially for Mrs Johnson. I'll be happier
if Tony Morton comes to see her. After all, she is his
patient. But, no, she'll come through.'

He looked down at her, and for a moment it was as
it had been before—the closeness of working together
and the growing personal closeness between the two of
them. And then, in a moment, the warmth in his eyes
was gone and the new hostility had returned.

'Thank you, Sister,' he said, formally, politely. He
looked at his watch. 'You're late going off duty. No
need for you to wait any longer.'

Thus dismissed, there was nothing Julie could do but
leave him and go on to the end of the corridor and up
the staircase to her small flat.

I don't know if I can go on like this, she thought with
sadness. Maybe I should resign, go back to Durban and
just forget I ever met Adam Brent.

Adam—and his children.

Forgetting them would not be easy, she knew very
well. But to go on like this—seeing Adam every day,
seeing the bewilderment on Catherine's face and on
David's because she had stopped spending time with
them—she didn't think she could bear that.

And yet to leave, to go away—Adam would be all
the more certain that he had been right about her all

along. As if that mattered, considering he could hardly think any worse of her.

But, when she got right down to it, there were her patients—the people who had come to depend on their Sister Sunshine. Miss Clifford, Captain O'Connor, Mrs Johnson, Ted Ramsay, Mrs Elliott.

I can't do it, Julie thought with certainty. I can't just walk out on them.

A little to her own surprise, she found that she was becoming very fond of Mark's grandmother. The old lady was a little imperious and a little demanding, but she was as independent as possible, she was entertaining and she was perceptive.

'You're looking as if you have something on your mind, Sister,' she said a few days later. 'In fact, if that old Casanova along the corridor hadn't told me they called you Sister Sunshine I wouldn't have guessed.' She smiled, taking any possible sting from her words, and then her voice was unexpectedly gentle.

'It seems to me, my dear, that my grandson might be responsible for some of the cloud on that sunshine. Could that be true?'

Julie hesitated. Mrs Elliott patted her hand.

'Now, I'm putting two and two together and perhaps coming up with five, or even six, but I've been thinking about Mark and his appendix and Cheryl being away and—Well, I can't help wondering if Mark was completely straight with you before Cheryl came back. If you knew he was engaged, I mean.'

Julie knew that her heightened colour gave the answer to that.

'I thought so,' Mrs Elliott said, nodding. She sighed. 'I love my grandson dearly but, at the same time, I know him very well. I can guess the rest. It suited him very nicely to have a pleasant little interlude with his pretty nurse, and just to keep quiet about his engagement.'

A pleasant little interlude, Julie thought. Yes, looking
back, she could see very well that that was what it had
been for Mark. And she could see, too, the truth of her
own feelings for him. He was so good-looking, all the
nurses thought he was wonderful and, yes, she had
known even while he was her patient that she was the
one he was attracted to. And when he had asked her to
meet him, that day he was discharged, and all the other
girls had been green with envy—

I thought I had fallen in love with him, Julie thought
wonderingly. But it wasn't love at all. I was flattered to
be the one he had chosen. What was that old song her
mother loved? Something about love and fascination—
that was all it had been. She could see it clearly now—
now that she knew how it felt to love someone.

'It's long enough ago now, Mrs Elliott,' she said. And
went on, because the old lady deserved her honesty, 'I
was pretty hurt at the time, but I got over it.' She smiled.
'Like you, I see Mark pretty clearly now.'

But Mark's grandmother hadn't finished. 'You mean
that, I can see,' she said thoughtfully. 'So you weren't
too bothered when Mark reappeared in your life.' And
then, taking Julie by surprise, she went on, 'But I'm
sure it did bother you that Mark used the fact that he
knew you to pull strings, to influence people on the
board, so that he could get me in here.'

'No, I didn't like that,' Julie agreed carefully, for Mrs
Elliott's blue eyes were much too searching.

'And I gather from Mark,' his grandmother went on
remorselessly, 'that Dr Brent was very angry to find
Mark kissing you the other day.'

Julie coloured. 'It wasn't very professional,' she said
quickly, defensively. 'There was nothing in it, really,
but Dr Brent thought—he got the impression—' Her
voice trailed away.

'He might have thought that you and Mark were

still involved?' Mrs Elliott suggested.

When Julie didn't reply, she nodded. 'I thought so,' she said, and now the sympathy in her voice was almost Julie's undoing. 'My dear, I may be an old woman but I'm not blind, and I've been watching the two of you. You are so careful, both of you so correct, so professional—but there is an atmosphere like a charge of electricity between you in the way you are so polite to each other and the way you avoid looking at each other.'

'Mrs Elliott—' Julie began, dismayed, not quite sure what she wanted to say. For a moment the old lady's hand covered hers.

'Don't worry, I don't think anyone else notices as much as I do. Or feels as responsible. Because I am pretty sure that whatever trouble there is between you and Dr Brent has been caused by my grandson. Am I right, Sister Maynard? Julie?'

There was nothing Julie could do but admit the truth.

'Yes, Mrs Elliott,' she said, her voice steady. 'Yes, you're right.'

The old lady sighed. 'And you don't want to talk about it, I suppose.'

'No, I don't,' Julie said, her voice low. Because talking about it wouldn't—couldn't—do any good. Whatever there had been between Adam and her was over.

And there was nothing she could do but accept that.

CHAPTER NINE

ONCE Julie had made her mind up that her real and her only priority was to her patients she was determined that she would have to learn to live with seeing Adam and working with him, although both of them were behaving like strangers.

No, she sometimes thought, worse than strangers. For strangers had never known each other—never been anything but strangers—while she and Adam had, for that short time, been so much more to each other.

Although she could and did talk to the children and spent a little time with them when they came to the verandah to visit the patients she could do no more than that, and she thought sometimes that it was like a physical ache to see the disappointment on David's face and the tears in Catherine's eyes when once again she had to refuse to come to the cottage to visit them.

She had another invitation from her friends in Camps Bay, and she went out to a film with the young accountant but, more and more, she found that she would rather spend her time off duty alone. Determinedly she reminded herself that she needed to catch up on her letter-writing, and she wrote to her family and to friends.

One night there was a phone call from Meg, in reply to her letter.

'I feel terrible,' Meg said, and Julie's heart lifted at Meg's usual drama-queen approach. 'I haven't written or even phoned since we got back from our Cape Town visit. I've neglected you horribly!'

Julie reassured her that it wasn't that bad, and that it didn't actually need sackcloth and ashes.

'No, but I could at least have phoned,' Meg said.

'So could I,' Julie pointed out, but her friend hardly heard her as she took a deep breath and started off again.

'But, Julie, you will never guess, not in a hundred years, why I've been so caught up,' Meg said.

'A man?' Julie hazarded.

'Well, of course,' Meg replied, surprised. 'But—but, Julie, after all these years of being friends, of being good chums, of crying on each other's shoulders over different love affairs. Julie, it's Ryan! Can you believe it?'

'Since you're telling me, yes, I can,' Julie said, laughing. 'Meg, I'm delighted. Are you making any plans?'

'Boy, are we making plans! Julie, we're talking marriage, we're talking engagement rings, white weddings—don't laugh, now—the whole tutti. No, we haven't set a date, but you have to come and be my bridesmaid.'

Julie promised that she would, and Meg said that as soon as a date had been set she would let Julie know. Then, as she was about to ring off, she said, 'Hey, Julie, you never did tell me any more about your doctor.'

'He isn't *my* doctor,' Julie returned, more sharply than Meg deserved. 'And there's nothing to tell.'

She then said goodbye, and put the phone down. No, there was nothing to tell.

But a few days later, when Adam had finished his round, he said to her stiffly, 'Sister Maynard, I have something to ask you.' He went on quickly, as if, Julie thought later, it was something that he had to get done with. 'You may remember Catherine talking about what she wants to do on her birthday. I've tried to persuade her to have a party and I've offered all sorts of other ideas, but she has her heart set on this.'

He looked down at her.

'Could you, just for one evening, put other things

aside and—come with us?' he said with difficulty. 'It would mean a great deal to Catherine.'

Julie's immediate instinctive feeling was that she couldn't do it; that it was asking too much. But Catherine's birthday—

She was never sure, afterwards, whether she agreed entirely for Catherine's sake or whether, deep down, she couldn't refuse the chance of this time with Adam, and with his children.

Stiffly, awkwardly, they made arrangements, and two nights later Julie ran down the steps of Halvey House to the waiting car.

She wished Catherine a happy birthday, and gave her the small parcel she had wrapped up that afternoon.

'It's a little friend for my Blue Ted,' Catherine said, delighted. 'He'll love that, Julie, cos he must get lonely sometimes.'

Both she and David talked eagerly, and Julie was glad of that because their chatter covered any awkwardness between Adam and her. But when they got out of the car at the cable station his eyes met hers, and there was something in the way he looked at her, something different, that made her heart turn over.

The ride in the cable-car on the warm summer evening was magic, with Table Mountain floodlit above them and the lights of the city, between the mountain and the sea, spread out and receding below them. The top of the mountain was well lit, and the paths were easy to follow.

Adam had booked a table in the small stone cottage restaurant and they went there right away, pausing only to admire the small furry dassies at the side of the path.

'Catherine has asked for hamburgers,' Adam said, 'but if there's anything else on the menu you'd rather have, just say.'

'I love hamburgers,' Julie replied truthfully.

'And chips,' David said, and she agreed that chips were necessary.

Once again, as in the car, the children's talking helped what could have been a difficult time. But Julie, from time to time, found Adam's grey eyes resting on her with an expression that she couldn't understand.

It was only when they left the restaurant and walked along the wide path towards the far end of the mountain 'table', with the children a little ahead of them, that Adam said abruptly, 'Julie, I was talking to Mrs Elliott today. Or rather, she was talking to me.' He looked down at her. 'She told me just what the position is between you and her grandson,' he said with difficulty. 'She told me, too, that I had been very hasty, not giving you the benefit of the doubt and not believing you when you told me it was over between you. But when I saw him kissing you—'

Julie took a deep and steadying breath.

'I wanted to tell you, to explain,' she said shakily, 'but I didn't know how to.'

'And I really made it impossible for you,' Adam said. 'Julie—'

Suddenly, his bleeper went off imperiously.

'Damn!' Adam said forcibly. 'I'll have to phone from the restaurant.'

'We'll follow you back,' Julie said as he turned and hurried back along the path.

She called to the children. 'Catherine—David—we have to go back. Your daddy's been bleeped, and he has to phone.'

They were further ahead than she had realised, she saw with some dismay.

'Julie, I can see some dassies down here, and I think they have babies,' Catherine called. 'I just want to see them.'

'No, Catherine,' Julie said sharply. 'Don't go near the edge.'

It was too late. Suddenly, terrifyingly, Catherine screamed, and a moment later David followed suit. Julie reached him before his scream had ended.

'Stand there—don't move,' she told him. She ran to the edge, and knelt down. Even with the moonlight and the floodlighting, it seemed an eternity before she saw the small huddled figure on a ledge below her.

'Catherine,' she said, and she tried to keep her voice steady, 'stay quite still.' She could see that any movement could take the child over the edge of the ledge she had mercifully fallen on.

'My leg hurts,' Catherine said, her voice blurred. 'And my head feels funny.'

There wasn't even a moment of conscious thought or decision. Julie turned to David.

'David, go right back along this big path,' she said very steadily, 'to the restaurant where we had the hamburgers. Your daddy is there. Tell him Catherine has fallen over the edge, and tell him I'm climbing down to her.'

The small boy's eyes were wide and his lips were trembling, but he nodded. Julie bent and hugged him quickly.

'Hurry, David,' she told him.

She was glad that she had put on flat shoes for walking on top of the mountain as climbing down was far from easy. More than once she felt her foot slipping, and she froze until she could find a safer foothold. The ledge Catherine had fallen onto wasn't very far down, but she could see that there was a sheer drop below it. It seemed an eternity before she reached the huddled little figure and found, to her relief, that the ledge was less narrow than it had looked from above.

Catherine was crying quietly and desperately but she

became calmer when Julie put her arms around her,
being very careful to keep the child as still as possible
until she could try to find out how and where she
was hurt.

'It's all right, Catherine,' she murmured. 'We'll just
stay here, you and I, until your daddy comes. Now, just
lie perfectly still and don't move at all.' As if we have
any choice about staying here, she thought, and fought
down the growing panic that thought brought.

She didn't dare to move enough to examine
Catherine's leg, but the awkward angle of her neck and
her complaint that her head was sore worried Julie more
than anything. Somehow she had to keep the little girl
very still, in case there was any injury to her neck.

'Julie! I'm coming down.'

It was Adam, peering down from above them.

'No, Adam, there isn't room,' Julie told him. 'I—I
think we have to be very careful about moving
Catherine. I'm telling her to keep still.'

He would understand, she knew.

'They've sent for the Mountain Rescue team,' Adam
said after a moment and, knowing him so well, she could
hear the effort he had to make to keep his voice steady
and calm. 'Don't worry, Catherine, just do what Julie
says and keep still.'

'I'm sorry, Daddy,' Catherine managed to say. 'I just
wanted to see if the dassies had babies, and—and then
I slipped.'

'It's all right, pet, I understand,' Adam said and, even
with that unbridgeable distance between where he was
and the ledge, Julie could hear the anguish in his voice.
'Just lie still. We'll get you up—you and Julie.'

It seemed to Julie that it was a lifetime that she and
Catherine were there on that ledge, her arms holding
the little girl steady and as still as possible. She hardly
dared to let herself think of the possible damage to

Catherine's neck and her spine. The summer night was warm, but occasionally she found herself shivering.

Adam talked at times—sometimes to them and sometimes to David beside him. Julie, on the ledge below, heard him talking to David but couldn't hear what he was saying. And suddenly she had an unbearable need for contact with him.

'Adam?' she called, and felt Catherine move in her arms. 'What's happening? Are—are they coming soon?'

'We called the Mountain Rescue team,' Adam told her. 'Mr Hilton from the restaurant came along with me, and went back to report to them exactly where you and Catherine are and—what might be needed. Wait a minute—I think this is him coming back now.'

A few moments later there was the sound of voices, and another man leaned over the edge.

'You all right there?'

'As right as we can be,' Julie replied, unable to keep her voice from shaking.

'The Mountain Rescue team are coming by helicopter. They should be here soon,' the man said. 'They'll land up here, and climb down to you.'

Catherine, barely conscious now, stirred and Julie told her what was happening, not even sure that the child could take it in.

And once again time slowed down, and the waiting seemed endless. Her arms were stiff and cramped, but she dared not loosen her grip on Catherine; dared not let her move, in case there was spinal damage.

What seemed like hours later Julie heard the sound of the helicopter. Distant, but getting closer. Then she could see it in the sky above, coming in to land. There was a deafening sound and a rush of air, followed by silence.

And after that, voices. Voices from the edge, where Adam was.

'Julie? They're coming down now.'

She closed her eyes, unable to watch the men climbing down and ridiculously afraid for them as they manoeuvred a stretcher down. But they knew what they were doing, and as they got closer she could see that they were roped for safety.

'It's all right, miss, we'll take the little girl,' the first man said.

'Be careful—I think her neck may be hurt,' Julie told him.

'It's all right. We're putting a neck brace on before we move her,' he said. 'Now, just you let go of her.'

Her arms were so stiff that it hurt to release her hold on Catherine. She watched as the rescue team expertly fitted a neck brace, and got Catherine onto the stretcher. Then, with one of them steadying the stretcher, it was raised to the top.

'Now for you. You're stiff and you're cramped so we'll put you in a sling.'

Now that she could see that the stretcher had reached the top Julie wouldn't have argued with them about anything. She let herself be strapped into the sling, and then she was steadily drawn upwards to safety. Her legs would have given way when she tried to stand but Adam was there, his arms around her to hold her steady.

'Catherine?' Julie said.

'She's in the helicopter. It's a big one—they can take us too. There's an ambulance waiting to take us to the Clinic,' Adam said.

Julie could remember very little of the journey in the helicopter, but there were fragments that were suddenly clear. Catherine's small form, so still, with the neck brace. David's voice as he asked his father if Catherine was all right. Adam's face, still and white in a sudden flare of light from the floodlit mountain.

Then the landing, and the transfer to the ambulance, and the strange, night-time stillness of the clinic as she sat with her arm around David, waiting.

Waiting.

She had thought that the wait on that mountain ledge had seemed endless, but it was nothing compared to the eternity since Catherine had been wheeled away. Adam had gone with her, and Julie sat with her arm around David. Someone brought tea and she drank a cup gratefully, but the little boy had fallen asleep and she didn't disturb him. Gently she moved him so that his head was on her lap and his feet on the couch.

It was only after she had drunk the tea that she realised how exhausted she was. But it didn't matter. Nothing mattered but Catherine, and knowing how badly hurt she was.

Some time during that long night Adam came back. In the bright light of the waiting-room she saw how grey and weary he looked. With no thought for anything but that, she held out one hand to him and he took it, his hand gripping hers hard.

'They're waiting for the X-rays now,' he told her. 'They'll come and tell us as soon as they can. I—needed to see how you and David were.'

'David's asleep,' Julie said unnecessarily, as he looked at the small copper head on her lap.

He sat down beside her, and the waiting was less hard, she thought, when they were together.

'Adam?' It was a doctor a little older than Adam, and he was holding X-ray plates in his hand. Adam stood up.

'Cervical trauma, but no fracture,' the doctor said. 'We'll have to put her in traction to relieve pressure on the nerve roots, and she may have to wear a collar afterwards for a while. The leg—she's been lucky; it isn't broken.' For the first time he smiled.

'In fact, I'd say she's been pretty lucky all round, considering. She's pretty heavily sedated now, and we're putting her in traction. Why don't you go home, and come back in the morning? There isn't much left of the night, but you all look as if you could do with some sleep—apart from the little fellow.'

Someone, and it didn't seem to matter who it was, had driven Adam's car from the cable station where they had left it—so long ago, it seemed—and brought it to the Clinic. As Adam drove through the quiet streets, with Julie holding David on her lap, the first light of dawn was streaking the sky.

Without asking her, he drove straight to the cottage. Gently he took the sleeping child from her. Julie followed him through the house. The big golden dog padded beside them, seeming to know that something was far from right.

Adam laid David down and covered him with a light duvet. Shandy, unbidden, settled himself on the rug beside the bed, nose on paws, on guard.

Adam looked at Julie.

'I think we need a cup of tea,' he said, 'before I take you back to the big house.'

Julie felt the beginnings of slightly hysterical laughter.

'I think I'm awash with tea,' she told him. 'People kept bringing it to me at the Clinic.'

She looked at him.

'But *you* need some tea,' she said.

And, in spite of what she had said, she made tea for both of them. They sat in the lounge in the early morning light, both of them beyond words—beyond the need or the ability to speak.

Then, after a long time, Adam put his cup down and looked at her.

'I started to tell you, on the mountain,' he said, with obvious difficulty, 'that I had been speaking to Mrs

Elliott. Julie, Julie, I should have known—I should have trusted you.'

Yes, Julie thought soberly, yes, Adam, you should have. But she knew so well how difficult it was for him to trust, and she could understand.

'Can you ever forgive me?' Adam said, taking both her hands in his.

'Forgive you?' she repeated, startled. As if there could be any doubt about that, ever. And then, unsteadily, she said, 'Oh, Adam, whatever there is to forgive, of course I can.'

It was like coming home to be in his arms again, with the distance and the differences gone. He kissed her gently and undemandingly, and for both of them it was enough just to be together.

'Come on,' Adam said after a long time, and she could hear the release of tension in his voice. 'I'd better take you back. It's almost morning.'

She shook her head.

'I'm not going back,' she said, her voice muffled against his shoulder. 'Please, Adam, I just want to stay here with you.'

'Julie, love,' he said, and the tenderness in his voice made her heart turn over, 'you're exhausted; you need to get to bed.'

She lifted her head. 'So let's go to bed,' she said. 'You're exhausted too.'

There was just a hint of laughter in his voice as he asked, 'Are you making advances to me, woman?'

She shook her head.

'Not this time,' she told him truthfully. 'I just—I just don't want to leave you, Adam.' He held her closer.

'And I don't want you to,' he said, not quite steadily.

He kissed the top of her head.

'Right now,' he said, his voice low, 'I'm too darned tired to do much about it so, yes, let's go to bed.'

There would be time to think—time to plan. For now, Julie knew, all she needed was for them just to be together.

CHAPTER TEN

THE sun was streaming into the bedroom when Julie awoke.

Adam wasn't there, and she pulled on his towelling gown and padded barefoot to the kitchen.

David was sitting at the table, eating cornflakes, and Adam was just putting the phone down.

'She's still sedated,' he said, answering her unspoken question. 'I said we'd go down as soon as possible so that we can be there when she does begin to surface.'

'Hi, Julie,' David said, unsurprised at seeing her there. 'I was scared when Catherine fell, but wasn't the helicopter great?'

Adam shook his head. 'He's been talking of nothing but the helicopter and the Mountain Rescue team,' he said. And then, smiling at his small son, he added, 'At least, once he knew Catherine was all right.'

'Do you know, Julie,' David said, as bright-eyed as if he had had a full night's sleep, 'Catherine will have to stay in hospital, and she'll miss school, an' when she does come home she'll have to wear a thing called a collar to make her neck better. But it isn't like Shandy's collar, of course, it's a collar what doctors use.'

'Of course,' Julie agreed gravely. For a moment Adam's eyes met hers, and there was the warm and intimate memory of falling asleep in his arms, each of them needing no more then than the comfort of being together.

'Adam,' she said, suddenly remembering, 'your call—when you went back to the restaurant—what did you do about it?'

'Told someone there to phone Tony Morton back, tell him what had happened and ask him to find another anaesthetist for his emergency op,' Adam told her.

Without asking her, he pushed a plate towards her.

'Tea and toast,' he told her. 'No time for anything more.' And then he added, heart-touchingly uncertain, 'That's if you want to come with us to see Catherine?'

'Of course I do,' Julie said, pouring herself a cup of tea. So much had happened in such a short time that she had to remind herself that it was Saturday, and she was off duty.

'Will Catherine be all bandaged up?' David asked when they were in the car.

'She'll have some bandages on,' Adam told him. 'And she'll have this special thing I was telling you about on her neck and her head to help her neck to get better.'

But a great deal of the little boy's exuberance and interest disappeared when they went into the ward where Catherine lay, her neck in traction and her leg bandaged. Julie felt David's hand creep into hers and she saw all the colour drain from his small face, leaving the freckles standing out.

'I don't like seeing Catherine like that,' he said shakily. 'I thought she would be sitting up in bed an' —an' she isn't even awake.'

'It's all right, David,' she reassured him. 'The doctors have given her something to make her sleep really soundly, but she'll begin to wake up soon.'

Adam had gone to talk to the doctor who was in charge and Julie, still with David's hand clutching hers, sat down at the side of the bed. It wasn't easy to look at Catherine professionally and with detachment, but she did think that the little girl was beginning to come out of the heavy sedation.

Adam came in then, and pulled up another chair.

'There isn't anything that's giving them any real concern,' he told her, his voice low. 'Her ankle is sprained and her knee is badly cut—it needed stitches. The cervical disc trauma was the most worrying thing, but there are no signs of any spinal damage so it will just be a matter of time.'

They were silent again, watching the unconscious child. But it was another half-hour before Catherine's eyelids flickered, and she murmured something. Julie, who was closest to her, bent nearer to hear her.

'I just wanted to see if the dassies had babies,' Catherine murmured. 'I'm sorry, Daddy.'

Adam leaned closer to her. 'I know you're sorry, Catherine,' he said, softly. 'We'll talk about it later.' They sat a little longer and then, seeing that Catherine was asleep again, they left her.

'She's just sleeping, son,' Adam reassured David. 'She'll feel better when she wakes next.'

'Are you angry with Catherine, Daddy?' David asked as they went along the corridor to the lift.

Adam hesitated.

'Not angry, no,' he said after a while. 'But when she's better we'll have to talk about it because it was a very dangerous thing to do, and Catherine could have been hurt much more than she is. Julie could have been hurt, too. And because Catherine was foolish the men from the Mountain Rescue team had to come out.'

There was a long silence, then David sighed.

'I'm glad it was Catherine what did it, not me,' he said with heartfelt relief.

They went back that afternoon to see Catherine, and she was awake—aware enough for Adam to talk to her about what she had done. Julie's heart went out to the little girl, biting her lip as she listened to her father, but she knew that Adam was right. These things had to be said. And when it was over Adam put his arms around her as best he could with the traction, and comforted her.

The next day Adam's parents came through from Stellenbosch after Adam had phoned them to tell them what had happened. Julie stayed at the cottage with David so Catherine wouldn't have too many visitors, and Adam brought his parents back there from the clinic.

'I'm glad I've seen her for myself,' his mother said, taking the cup of tea Julie handed to her. 'I was so worried when Adam phoned, and I must say it isn't nice seeing her in traction like that, but it could have been so much worse.' Her eyes met Julie's. 'Adam told me what you did, my dear. He says she could have fallen off that ledge or she could have hurt her neck more if you hadn't climbed down and held her still.'

'I don't even want to think about that now,' Julie admitted.

Mrs Brent patted her hand. 'I'm just so glad you were there, Julie. For Catherine, and for Adam.' That was all she said, but it was enough. And, when she and Adam's father left, she put her arms around Julie and kissed her cheek. 'Come and see us soon, my dear,' she said. 'You and Adam, and the children.'

'We'll come when Catherine gets out of hospital, Mum,' Adam promised. 'Maybe before that.' He put one arm around Julie's shoulders, lightly but yet—Julie thought wonderingly—so possessively.

And later, when David was asleep, he said to her, 'We need to talk, Julie.'

And they did start out by talking—sensibly, practically. Explanations—apologies—promises—plans.

Then, in the middle of it, Adam was all at once silent. He looked at her, his grey eyes dark and questioning. Julie could feel her heart thudding unevenly.

He said her name once, unevenly. And then they were in each other's arms and there were no reservations, no hesitation—nothing but total commitment as he kissed

her, gently at first and then not at all gently. For the
first time there was no need for Julie to fight against
the eager response of her whole body to the urgent and
searching demand of his arms and his lips.

Later—how much later, she neither knew nor cared—
she stirred in his arms.

'What were we talking about before we got—side-
tracked?' she murmured, knowing very well what they
had been talking about.

Gently, with one finger, he traced the outline of
her mouth.

'I think,' he said softly, 'I was asking you how soon
we could get married.'

'Yes, I thought that was it,' Julie agreed demurely.
And then, not quite steadily, she gave him his answer.
'As soon as possible, Adam.'

They would have to wait, they agreed, until Catherine
was out of hospital and free from the collar she would
have to wear. Then Adam suggested that Julie might
want the wedding to be in Durban, where her family
and friends were. But Julie shook her head.

'My family will come to Cape Town,' she told Adam,
'and so will some of my friends.' She looked up at him.
There was a tiny chapel on the ground floor of the
hospital. It seemed so right that they should be married
there in Halvey House.

Adam, when she suggested this, liked the idea. The
minister from the church just down the road would marry
them, he said. Both he and Julie knew him as he held
a service once a week in the chapel, and always went
round the patients afterwards.

'Do you think we've dealt with all these practical
things?' Adam said, drawing her closer to him. 'Because
if we have—'

And once again it was a long, long time before they
drew apart, Adam murmuring—his mouth close to her

ear—that they had a lot of lost time to make up.

'I think we're doing a pretty good job on that,' Julie told him, laughing.

There was no point, they decided, in trying to keep their changed relationship a secret. But certain people had to be first to know.

The next day Julie phoned her parents. To her amazement, her mother wasn't only delighted but unsurprised.

'I thought there was something between you and Adam,' she said.

'But I've hardly mentioned him,' Julie replied.

'Yes, that's why I wondered,' her mother returned. And then she went on, 'Just let us know when you set the date, and Dad and I and the boys will be there. And Gran too, of course there'll be no keeping her away.'

Adam's parents, too, were pleased. And also unsurprised.

'I hoped so much that first time, Julie,' Adam's mother said, hugging her. 'And I was so disappointed when things didn't seem to be working out.'

A little later Julie saw her talking quietly to Adam. Adam smiled and then his mother left the room. When she came back she had a small velvet box in her hand, which she gave to Adam.

'This was my grandmother's ring, Julie, and I think it might have been her mother's,' Adam said, giving her the box. 'Mum asked if I'd got you a ring and I said not yet, so—she wondered if you'd like to have this one.'

Julie opened the box. The ring was a broad band of gold, with tiny sapphires and diamonds set into it. Her gasp of delight made words unnecessary, and Adam took her left hand and put the ring on it. It fitted as if it had been made for her.

'No one has worn it since my grandmother died ten years ago,' Adam told her, and she knew that what he was really saying was that this ring was hers—that Celia had never owned it.

David and his grandfather and the dogs came in just then.

'See this ring your daddy has just given Julie?' his grandmother said to David. 'This means that Daddy and Julie are going to be married.'

'I thought so,' the little boy said, nodding. 'Cos they're always kissing. Can we tell Catherine when we visit her this afternoon? And can I have another crunchie biscuit, Gran?'

Catherine's neck was still in traction, but her eyes widened and her smile told them that she liked the idea.

'But you won't get married until I'm better, will you?' she said anxiously, and Julie assured her that they wouldn't.

Matron, although more reserved, was also pleased with the news.

'Does this mean we're losing our Sister Sunshine?' she asked.

'No, of course not,' Julie said immediately.

'We haven't talked about it, but I shouldn't think so,' Adam said at the same time. And then, warm teasing in his voice, he went on, 'Not for quite a while, anyway.'

The usual hospital grapevine worked and somehow, without either Adam or Julie actually telling anyone, everyone seemed to know.

Mrs Elliott, in particular, seemed to feel that most of the credit was due to her. And perhaps rightly, Julie thought, although now it seemed inconceivable that she and Adam could have remained apart. But, yes, they certainly should feel grateful to Mrs Elliott.

'I just thought Dr Brent needed a bit of a talking-to,' she said to Julie. 'And since I felt responsible, thanks

to that grandson of mine, it did seem only right that I
should do what I could.'

Little Miss Clifford's cheeks were pink with
excitement.

'It's so wonderful to see Dr Brent looking happy
again, my dear,' she said to Julie. 'The two of you are
so right for each other. When Dr Brent smiled at you
just now, Sister, it just reminded me of—of someone I
knew long ago.'

Her eyes were misty, and when Julie left her she was
still smiling and was planning to write to Mrs Smit
to tell her.

'Well, it's certainly one way of making sure we don't
lose our Sister Sunshine,' Captain O'Connor said
gruffly. 'Marry the girl, and keep her here!' But, beneath
his fierce eyebrows, his eyes were twinkling.

Ted Ramsay was equally delighted.

'Linda will be so pleased too,' he told Julie. 'Mind
you, she's been saying for weeks that she'd like to see
the two of you getting together.'

Mrs Johnson admired Julie's ring—worn on a chain
round her neck when she was in uniform—and said that
when she thought of that night when she had been so
ill and Dr Brent and Sister Maynard had worked together
she was sure they would have a wonderful marriage.

There was an ecstatic phone call from Meg, whose
mother had heard from Julie's mother.

'But why didn't you phone right away to tell me?'
she demanded.

'I was going to,' Julie said truthfully, 'but I just
haven't had time. Either I'm working, or we're visiting
Catherine. So, who's getting married first, Meg,
you or me?'

It seemed that it would be Julie and Adam, and Meg
promised that she and Ryan would come to Cape Town
for the wedding.

Mark Elliott, visiting his grandmother, looked into the duty room as he was leaving.

'Gran's been telling me your news, Julie,' he said. He smiled, but something of the usual confidence was gone. 'She's been telling me, too, that I nearly messed things up for you. I'm sorry about that, Julie.'

For perhaps the first time he was completely serious as he looked down at her, his blue eyes very dark.

'I'm sorry about more than that,' he said, his voice low, 'but I guess it's too late to say that.

'Be happy, Julie,' he went on, not quite steadily. 'I hope your doctor knows that you're—pretty special.'

'I hope you'll be happy too, Mark,' Julie said, meaning it.

One night, as they came away from visiting Catherine— just the two of them because it was late for David and he was at home, with Beauty looking after him—Adam stopped, and looked down at Julie.

'All these plans,' he said quietly, 'and Catherine now, saying she wants to be a bridesmaid. We've never really talked about whether it's any problem for you—taking on the children, I mean. I shouldn't just be taking it for granted.'

His grey eyes were troubled.

'At one time,' Julie said slowly, because it was so important to say this the right way, 'I did wonder. Oh, that was early on when we spoke about you needing time. I felt that I needed some time, too, to be quite certain. But that day on the mountain, Adam, when we were waiting for the Mountain Rescue team Catherine was as much my child as if I had given birth to her. David too. I love them both dearly, Adam, and, no, it isn't a problem.'

But he didn't leave it there.

'They're not perfect, you know,' he said. 'You've

probably seen them at their best, but they can be annoy-ing, irritating, quarrelsome—you name it.'

'I'm sure they can,' Julie agreed. 'And they would be if I was their real mother. And—and any children you and I may have won't be perfect either.'

She stood on tiptoe and kissed him.

'I remember once hearing my mother and one of her friends talking,' she said, and she smiled. 'They were talking about their children, and my mother said, "Sometimes I don't like them very much, but I always love them." And I guess that's how it will be.'

When they got back to the cottage Beauty went home, and Adam and Julie—with Shandy padding along beside them—went to check on David.

'When is Catherine coming home?' he asked sleepily, as he did every day. But tonight they had an answer for him.

'The day after tomorrow,' Adam told him. 'She'll have to wear a collar for three or four weeks and she'll have physiotherapy, then she'll be better.'

'An' then we'll have the wedding,' David said. He looked up at Julie. 'Catherine said she was going to ask if she could be a bridesmaid or a flowergirl,' he said. 'She told me that yesterday when we were there.'

'She is going to be a bridesmaid,' Julie told him. 'She's going to wear a pretty dress, and carry a little bunch of flowers.'

The little boy looked alarmed. 'They don't have flowerboys, do they?' he asked. 'Or—or bridesboys?' Julie assured him that he wouldn't have to be a flowerboy.

'I'll just be there,' he agreed, sleepy again.

But when they had both kissed him goodnight he said, laughing, 'Couldn't Shandy be a flowerdog? Or a bridesdog, or something?' Adam and Julie left him, still murmuring the funny words to himself, with Shandy in his usual position on the rug beside the bed.

There was a hint of autumn in the air, and Adam went to close the big front door of the cottage. They stood outside on the stoep for a little while. The night sky was dark, with the moon hidden behind clouds and a heavy bank of cloud over Table Mountain.

'Summer is almost over,' Adam said softly.

It didn't matter, Julie thought. There will be another summer for Adam and me, and the children. There will be so many more summers.

All the rest of our lives.

Together.

COMING NEXT MONTH

NOT HUSBAND MATERIAL! by Caroline Anderson
Audley Memorial Hospital

Jill Craig was not impressed when the flirtatious, but very
handsome Zach Samuels breezed into the Audley and
proceeded to charm everyone—including herself! She could
not deny the intense desire that they both felt, but could she
trust him to love only her?

A CAUTIOUS LOVING by Margaret O'Neill

Dr Thomas Brodie was reluctant to hire Miranda Gibbs. Why
was such a beautiful, intelligent and diligent woman moving to
the country? But then he saw her in action as a nurse. Miranda
might get the job but she would never have his heart...

WINGS OF SPIRIT by Meredith Webber
Flying Doctors

Christa Cassimatis had known station owner Andrew Walsh
on a strictly professional basis for months, so she was
astonished when Andrew suddenly proposed! She barely
knew the man, and now he wanted to get married! She knew
it must be for all the wrong reasons...

PRESTON'S PRACTICE by Carol Wood

The name Preston Lynley rang alarm bells for Vanessa Perry!
But then Preston provoked the most surprising reactions,
including being incredibly attracted to him, from the minute
she had begun her new job at his Medical Practice! But he also
made Vanessa remember her tragic past—and his link to it...

MILLS & BOON®

Medical Romance™

Flying Doctors

Don't miss this exciting new mini-series from popular
Medical Romance author, Meredith Webber.

**Set in the heat of the Australian outback,
the Flying Doctor mini-series experiences
the thrills, drama and romance of life
on a flying doctor station.**

Look out for:

Wings of Spirit by Meredith Webber
in June '97

New York Times bestselling author

JAYNE ANN KRENTZ

Full Bloom

Part bodyguard, part troubleshooter, Jacob Stone
had, over the years, pulled Emily out of countless
acts of rebellion against her domineering family.
Now he'd been summoned to rescue her from a
disastrous marriage. Emily didn't want his
protection—she needed his love. But did Jacob
need this new kind of trouble?

"A master of the genre...nobody does it better!"

—Romantic Times

**AVAILABLE IN PAPERBACK
FROM MAY 1997**

FREE!

FOUR FREE
specially selected
Medical Romance™ novels
PLUS a FREE Mystery Gift
when you return this page...

Return this coupon and we'll send you 4 Medical Romance novels and a mystery gift absolutely FREE! We'll even pay the postage and packing for you.

We're making you this offer to introduce you to the benefits of the Reader Service™– FREE home delivery of brand-new Medical Romance novels, at least a month before they are available in the shops, FREE gifts and a monthly Newsletter packed with information, competitions, author profiles and lots more...

Accepting these FREE books and gift places you under no obligation to buy, you may cancel at any time, even after receiving just your free shipment. Simply complete the coupon below and send it to:

MILLS & BOON READER SERVICE, FREEPOST, CROYDON, SURREY, CR9 3WZ.

READERS IN EIRE PLEASE SEND COUPON TO PO BOX 4546, DUBLIN 24

NO STAMP NEEDED

Yes, please send me 4 free Medical Romance novels and a mystery gift. I understand that unless you hear from me, I will receive 4 superb new titles every month for just £2.20* each, postage and packing free. I am under no obligation to purchase any books and I may cancel or suspend my subscription at any time, and the free books and gift will be mine to keep in any case. (I am over 18 years of age)

M7XE

Ms/Mrs/Miss/Mr_____
BLOCK CAPS PLEASE

Address_____

_____

_____ Postcode _____

NEW YORK TIMES
BESTSELING AUTHOR

Anne
Mather

Dangerous Temptation

He was desperate to remember... Jake wasn't
sure why he'd agreed to take his twin brother's
place on the flight to London. But when he
awakens in hospital after the crash, he can't even
remember his own name or the beautiful woman
who watches him so guardedly. Caitlin. His wife.

She was desperate to forget...
Her husband seems like a stranger to Caitlin—a
man who assumes there is love when none exists.
He is totally different—like the man she'd thought
she had married. Until his memory returns.
And with it, a danger that threatens them all.

"Ms. Mather has penned a wonderful romance."
—Romantic Times

MIRA®

AVAILABLE IN PAPERBACK
FROM MAY 1997